assignment:
murder

She was a lovely lady reporter, tracking down a story. She came to this secluded mansion in search of the facts.

What she found was quite different—a twisted nightmare of terror, violence, and hatred.

There was a murderer loose, and she knew that unless she could discover the killer's identity, her curiosity was going to be the death of her . . .

"Absorbing"

—New York Times

"The best mystery I've read this year. It's got *something*"

—Norman Klein
New York Post

LESLIE FORD has become one of the most widely read mystery writers in America. Her first novel was published in 1928 and since then she has written around forty others.

Miss Ford lives in Annapolis, Maryland.

Among her books are *False To Any Man*, *Old Lover's Ghost*, *The Town Cried Murder*, *The Woman in Black*, *Trial By Ambush*, *Ill Met By Moonlight* and *The Simple Way of Poison*, all published in Popular Library editions.

the clue
of the
judas tree
by leslie ford

WILDSIDE PRESS

*the clue
of the
judas tree*

ONE

It was just noon when I came out of Mr. McCrae's office and bumped smack into Fate in one of its better disguises. He was tall and large and blond, and awfully good-looking, with gray eyes and a gravely humorous mouth. I know the last two points because he picked up my bag and smiled at me and said, "So sorry!" as if it wasn't entirely my fault. At least, that's what I thought until I looked up at him and saw the amused smile of a man ever so sure of himself and the effect he'd have on a woman if she just looked at him even once.

I suppose that's why I was a little disconcerted when I found him, two hours later, sitting across the aisle from me on the Congressional Limited I'd just caught as it pulled out of the Pennsylvania Station. He was looking at me with an amused quizzical twinkle in his eyes. I smiled, and he got up promptly and came over.

"You're going to Baltimore, I believe," he said.

"How did you know?"

"McCrae told me," he said. "May I sit here? I'm going there too."

"Really?"

I was a little pleased, but also a little alarmed. It was like having the Prince of Wales drop in for lunch when you'd planned on making peace with your diet for having dined at Pierre's the night before. But it was all settled, and the porter moved over his very swagger well-used luggage, with first-class steamer labels torn off except for just enough so you could see they had been red and white, and not blue. He settled himself—composing his long legs encased in misty-colored Irish tweed, and his feet in heavy pebbled English shoes, around my bags wasn't as simple as you'd think—and smiled at me, as much as to say all this was a lot of trouble but it was worth it, sitting next to me.

It took me a long time to find out that this very special way of his was part of his stock in trade, and that all women fell for it just as I was doing—the older the harder; and that it was all just a game with him. Except, of course, that he lived by it, and so I suppose it was really business and not pleasure. But that's being rather unfair. He had little or nothing to gain by being charming to me, unless he just liked to keep his hand in, as it were.

"I know all about you, you see," he said with a smile. "Your name's Louise Cather, you're a journalist, you're going to Ivy Hill, Chesapeake Bay estate of Duncan Trent, and you're going to write his autobiography. It will be entitled 'Life and What It has Meant to Me, by Duncan Trent, millionaire shipbuilder and capitalist extraordinary.' Right?"

"Quite," I said. "How did you know? Don't tell me you're something overwhelming in fortune tellers?"

"No, it's quite simple. I won't add 'Watson'—that's been overdone. McCrae told me you were coming on this train. Shall I tell you what he told me?"

"That all depends," I said.

"Oh, it was very complimentary. He said you had red hair, yellow-green eyes, and were one of the few intelligent women he knew who was really good-looking. As a matter of fact, I think he said beautiful—at least he should have. Then I knew all the rest because I came from Ivy Hill myself last week, and they were all talking about it. Trent has neglected everything trying to remember boyhood pranks to entertain your readers."

"That's bad," I said. "I'd rather he'd just be natural about it."

"How could he? Every self-made man feels he's got a lot to tell the rest of us so we'll get along and be millionaires too. Then it's rather flattering to have a ghost while you're still alive. Most of us have to wait till we're dead."

"I'm afraid he won't find me a very good ghost," I said. Usually you have to leave out the things people like the best about themselves, and they generally feel, when you've got through, that they could have done it much better if they'd had the time.

A sudden idea struck me.

"You're not Mr. Trent yourself, by the way, are you?"

He laughed, and when he did he threw back his fine blond head and really laughed.

"Lord, no!" he said. "I'm Victor Paul Sartoris, doctor of medicine and what not. Mrs. Trent is a patient of mine."

"Oh. Then you know them quite well?"

"Quite, I should say."

"Then tell me what Mr. Trent's like."

"Ah!" he said. "McCrae told me not to. He said I was to let you find out for yourself. Not to smudge up any first impressions."

Mr. McCrae is the editor of the magazine that was sending me to Ivy Hill to write Mr. Trent's own story for its two million readers.

"He's a great believer in first impressions," I said.

"In yours anyway. He said you had astonishing intuitions."

"Most of them too astonishing," I said. I remembered Mr. McCrae's final injunction, given me just before I bumped into Dr. Sartoris outside the door: "Now for God's sake, Louise, use your head and don't send me back a bunch of tripe."

"But I can tell you about the rest of them at Ivy Hill," he went on. He had one eyebrow raised a little, as if he hadn't much use for any of them.

"Are they as bad as all that?" I asked.

"Oh, on the contrary. They're delightful. At least, most of them are."

"How many are there, for heaven's sake?" I demanded.

"Well, you begin with Mr. and Mrs. Duncan Trent, self-made millionaire and his wife."

"That's simple."

"Not as simple as you'd think," he returned seriously. "It might be if it weren't that there's Agnes Hutton—she's Mr. Trent's secretary—and Major Ellicott, who's a sort of cousin or something."

"I take it we don't approve of Miss Hutton the secretary and Major Ellicott the cousin or something."

"Wrong again. I approve of them both. She's good-looking and clever—almost too clever, I'd say, for her own good. And while Ellicott isn't especially clever, he's decorative— rides, swims, shoots, dances, plays fine poker and contract. In short, Miss Cather, he's an officer and a gentleman, and I predict you'll fall in love with him before you've been at Ivy Hill a week."

"That's something to look forward to, anyway," I said. "Who else is there?"

"There's Perry Bassett. He's Mrs. Trent's brother. A sort of mental case, I suppose you'd call him. Æsthenic, you know. He's lost two fortunes in the market. Now he's emotionally worn out, and he grows roses and melons and wears an old brown hat with a hole in the top of it."

"I'll fall in love with him, I think, instead of Major Ellicott," I said.

He shook his head smilingly.

"No, because he's entirely concerned with his gardens. And his niece."

"Who's she?"

"She's Cheryl Trent. Age twenty, very lovely, very rich, very charming."

Dr. Sartoris spoke lightly; but there was something in his voice when he said that that caused me not to say what was on the tip of my tongue. I thought it was obvious that he was in love with Cheryl Trent. After all—very lovely, very rich, very charming: why not?

"And there's Mr. Archer. He's the family lawyer, guardian of Mr. Trent's income tax report and all the rest of it. You'll like him. He's a rotund, jovial old fellow with a finger in all the Trent and Spur Corporation pies."

Somehow, without being able to say just why, I got the definite impression that Dr. Sartoris did not like Mr. Archer.

"He doesn't properly live at Ivy Hill," he went on. "Has a place on a cove a little farther along the bay. But he spends most of his time at the Trents' place. You'll see a lot of him. I imagine he'll act as a sort of censor of what you write. That's his chief occupation."

Again, and again without being able to say why, I felt that there was a pretty strained relationship between the lawyer and the doctor. And I wondered why. I needn't have bothered, for I found out soon enough as it was.

We talked after that about one thing and another, until Dr. Sartoris took a paper out of his pocket and offered it to me.

"I've got a magazine, thanks," I said. I got it out from under my coat and turned to the story I wanted to read.

We'd crossed the Susquehanna and were roaring through Havre de Grace when I glanced up. I hadn't realized how far South we'd come. It was really spring in Maryland. Across the tilled fields the trees wore a bright aura of young green, and now and then there was a peach tree still in full pink blossom.

New York seemed a thousand miles away, and for a moment I had the queer empty feeling that I suppose amateur adventurers have when they've burned their last bridge, and there's nothing to do but go ahead. I glanced at Dr. Sartoris.

I thought of telling him something of the sort, until I saw he was reading the financial page and was frowning over something or other half-way down the latest quotations from Wall Street.

Pretty soon the names of Baltimore hotels and shops began to appear on the signboards along the way. Dr. Sartoris put his paper back in his overcoat pocket and got up.

"We'll be in shortly," he said. He reached in his jacket pocket and took out his handkerchief. As he did so the train gave a sudden jolt, and a folded yellow paper that had come along with his handkerchief, and hung for an instant on the edge of his pocket, jerked sharply out and fluttered to the floor at just the instant that he turned and started down the aisle. It came to a stop between our seats, and I reached down to pick it up. Before I realized it, the words

MICHAEL SPUR RETURNING COME AT
ONCE URGENT LOVE EMILY TRENT

caught my eye; and I realized then that in effect I had actually read it. I also found myself thinking that the girl's name was Cheryl—in which case "Emily" must be Mrs. Trent. But why the "love," and who was Michael Spur?

I didn't know just what to do. Obviously if Dr. Sartoris hadn't wanted the thing to remain a secret he would have mentioned Michael Spur. But he hadn't; and he certainly hadn't indicated that he and Mrs. Trent were on such friendly terms. The porter fortunately took the matter out of my hands. He had come for our baggage, and when he spotted the telegram and bent to pick it up I decided that was my cue to powder my nose and do something with lipstick. I left in the opposite direction.

When I came back Dr. Sartoris was there, and I couldn't discover anything in his frank, friendly, though rather amused smile that indicated any concern about his telegram. As a matter of fact, being a journalist gets one in rather bad habits about other people's affairs. I found myself inordinately curious about this man and Mrs. Trent and the mysterious Michael Spur.

The train slowed down and stopped, and the porter handed down our bags.

"There's Miss Trent now," Dr. Sartoris said, waving his hat. I looked past him and saw a very lovely girl, smiling and radiant.

11

"Hullo!" she cried.

"This is Miss Cather, Cheryl," said Dr. Sartoris—rather quickly, I thought.

Cheryl Trent turned to me. I saw chiefly a pair of wide-set deep blue eyes.

"Oh!" she said. "How do you do?"

TWO

I couldn't tell at the moment whether Cheryl Trent, blue-eyed, with a mass of shining curls showing under a jaunty little dark blue hat that matched her blue tweed suit with white piqué waistcoat and her blue slippers, resented my being there, or just my being there with Dr. Sartoris. She needn't have, certainly, because it was perfectly obvious that so far as the handsome blond doctor was concerned, only one woman existed at that moment.

I followed them up the steps and across the street to the large coffee-colored Cadillac that was being inspected by several red-caps and a couple of taxi-drivers. Dr. Sartoris opened the door.

"Will you ride in front with me, Miss Cather?" Cheryl Trent asked coolly.

"No, thanks," I said.

She looked a little startled, and Dr. Sartoris intervened promptly.

"I'll sit with you, Cheryl," he said. "Miss Cather's had enough of me for today—haven't you?"

"Quite," I said.

Cheryl glanced at him. I couldn't make out whether the girl was beautiful, but not particularly bright, or what. She seemed rather confused. I wondered a moment if she knew who I was, or thought I was just something Dr. Sartoris had picked up and brought along.

I got in, and the porter and Dr. Sartoris arranged the bags.

Cheryl Trent, at the wheel, leaned back.

"Do you mind putting that parcel up on the seat," she said. "It's something of Dad's and it might break."

I picked the parcel up off the floor. It felt like a box of writing paper, and not in the least fragile; but I deposited it carefully on the seat. I've often thought since then of that plain brown-paper-wrapped parcel, and its importance—so long unsuspected—in the events that occurred during my short stay at Ivy Hill.

I looked at Cheryl Trent with some curiosity as we went along. Whatever else she might or might not be able to do, she could certainly manage a motor car. It was little short of miraculous the way she slipped through the traffic on Baltimore's famous Charles Street—which is more like Bond Street at eleven o'clock in the morning than the leading thoroughfare in a wealthy American city. Again, when she passed a double-tanked oil trunk on a curve at the top of a hill on the Annapolis pike, and missed by about half-an-inch, and without batting a silky eyelash, six Negroes who were apparently rebuilding a Model-T Ford, I decided there was more to her than you'd think.

She obviously had something to say to Dr. Sartoris, and I was equally obviously in the way. I thought of pretending I was deaf, or something, but I gave it up when my eye happened to catch hers in the oblong mirror over the windshield. For an instant we regarded each other with calm impersonal appraisal. Before she dropped her eyes to the road, which she evidently knew well enough to drive blindfolded, there was something like a smile of acceptance in her face. And then she turned to Dr. Sartoris, who had been talking cheerfully about New York.

"Mother's been raising hell since you left," she said calmly.

"Really?"

I thought Dr. Sartoris was a little startled out of his complacement charm.

"Hutton's been simply poisonous. Mother'll cut her throat some day. If somebody else doesn't do it first."

"What's Agnes been doing?" he asked. He didn't glance back at me and say, "You see?—I told you so"; but he might just as well have.

"Oh, the usual things. Nothing you can take hold of and go to Dad and say 'Agnes Hutton said *this* to Mother, and you've got to fire her.' It's nothing like that. You simply *can't* say to Dad that Agnes kept calling the yew trees the Jew trees without making him laugh, and then he says it serves Mother right. She's always getting words wrong, and Agnes never does anything but smile, and then use them the first time there's anybody around. And the stuff Mother reads and thinks is Literature, and all that. You know how she makes fun of her, openly, all the time. About her having her face lifted, and all that sort of thing."

"I know," said Dr. Sartoris sympathetically.

14

"And you can't blame Mother for hating her, and being half-afraid of her at the same time," Cheryl went on. "Agnes is awfully clever, and attractive too, and she's so sweet to Dad it makes me sick at my stomach."

The determined sort of ruthless nonchalance in the girl's manner gradually disappeared.

"Of course really I don't give a rap about it. It's Mother's own fault. But she oughtn't to stand for it."

You could see that she did give a pretty big rap about it. I thought she was rather sweet, under this mask of not caring about anything.

"I'll talk to Agnes," Dr. Sartoris said gently.

"I wish you would," Cheryl said. "If you don't, *something's* going to happen—and it's mess enough with all this new business hanging over us."

Dr. Sartoris half-turned to look at her, slim and nonchalant, flicking cigarette ash out of the window with one small white-gloved hand.

"What new business?" he asked.

"Don't you know?"

Her voice had sunk, and instead of pretending I was deaf I found myself straining my ears to hear her above the smooth hum of the motor.

"About Michael Spur?" she went on.

Dr. Sartoris shook his head—or I *thought* he did.

"He's coming back."

Something like awe or dread, or just plain fear, sharpened the edges of her voice, which was normally rather husky and pleasant.

"When?"

"We don't know—that's the horrible part of it," she said quickly. "Today, tomorrow—we don't know. We're just living in terror of it. Mother's almost beside herself. Everybody's on edge. It's perfectly ghastly."

There was a long silence after that. We had left the dreary expanse of service stations and chicken coops, and were traveling swiftly through great banks of snowy-petaled dogwood.

A little cry of joy broke from Cheryl's smooth rouged lips.

"Isn't it *lovely!*"

Just ahead was a sudden deep red slash in the snowy mass. I saw her looking at it at the same time that I did; and she gave an involuntary shudder.

"What's that red stuff?" I asked practically.

"Judas Tree," she said softly. "It looks like blood, in the snow."

Dr. Sartoris smiled at her.

"I should say you *are* rather jumpy," he said, and she laughed a little. "I'm sorry," she said.

She turned to the right, and in a few moments turned again, into a narrow dirt road marked only by a couple of cylinders, with the names of Baltimore papers painted on them, perched on posts that were stuck at crazy angles into the ground. In a quarter of a mile or so we turned again, through a pair of beautifully wrought but rather medieval iron gates, between two brick pillars.

The unkempt dirt road had not prepared me for the gates —with a ducal crown worked in slender metal in the centers of them—nor for what was on the other side. Just ahead of us was a tiny lake, shimmering green and mauve and yellow in the setting sun. Three stately white swans moved idly across it to the shelter of a tall weeping willow with young green streamers gesturing gently in the dying breeze. Beyond stretched lawns and gardens and arbors and trees, and beyond them lay a silent bay opening into the broad waters of the Chesapeake. A slim white sail floated in the distance, and far beyond it a steamer with black smoke coming from its funnel moved down the Bay. From the car window I saw a screen of pollarded cedars, and beyond it a house. A very astonishing house.

Just why I had assumed that Ivy Hill would be red brick and Georgian, I don't know. I suppose it was because I hadn't met Mrs. Trent. It wasn't red brick, and it wasn't Georgian. It was pink brick and tile, and it was frankly and appallingly Tudor Gothic, with high arched windows and flattened flying buttresses. It was an extraordinary building, and it must have cost tons of money.

Dr. Sartoris turned back to me as we came up to it.

"The Trents built this place before the present interest in the Early American," he said. "The decorators scoured Europe to keep it in period, but fortunately Mrs. Trent has great independence of spirit."

Something like a plain grunt came from the girl at his side.

I got the idea that they were preparing me for the worst.

And in its way the house at Ivy Hill was as incredible as the things that happened in it. In fact, I suppose, it was the kind of house that strange things have to happen in, as a sort of ironic destiny. I didn't, of course, know any of that when Cheryl Trent brought the big car to a stop in front of an elaborate oak studded door. A colored butler, white-haired, in plum-colored livery, greeted Cheryl with a broad grin.

"Is yo' back, Miss Cherry?" he squeaked in a pleased falsetto. Then he bowed to Dr. Sartoris.

"We didn' speck yo', suh."

Dr. Sartoris smiled genially.

"I came quite suddenly," he said.

"We's always mighty glad to have yo', suh."

"This is Miss Cather, Magothy," said Cheryl.

"Evenin', miss."

I handed him Cheryl's parcel and got out. I had a brief chance to look around while he was sorting my baggage from Dr. Sartoris's. It was then that I decided it was an incredible place and that incredible things could easily happen there; in fact, a strange thing happened almost immediately. I was looking up at the tall narrow leaded windows when I saw a curtain just above us fall suddenly—not suddenly enough, however, to keep me from seeing a woman's hand making elaborate signals to one of us there in the drive. I looked around. Cheryl was busy, with her back to the house; and as for Dr. Sartoris, his gray eyes and fine clear-cut features were as bland and innocent as you please. In fact, he was looking the other way too. I had a curious feeling of something out of the way going on; but Magothy's high amused cackle at something Cheryl said to him seemed so innocent and friendly that I decided it was the large pink building with the queer leaded windows that was doing it. It was incongruous enough, Heaven knows, there by the clear smiling waters of the Chesapeake.

"We dine at seventy-thirty, Miss Cather," Cheryl Trent was saying to me. "Aspasia will be up there to show you the ropes, and I'll be along before dinner."

I said "Thanks," and followed Magothy inside, into an enormous high-ceilinged hall, paneled in dark mellow oak, with a wide staircase going up ahead of us and a balcony running around three sides of it. The staircase had three suits of armor, two holding spears, stationed on the landing. The balcony rail was hung for all the world like the chapel in Les Invalides, with tattered banners of faded blue and gold and red. The only thing missing was a tomb in the center of the floor below, and we got that before we were through with it. The whole place was dimly lighted through the high windows, but warmly lighted—there was a rose window over the landing.

"Them armors is from Europe," Magothy said, pointing to the mailed figures. "An' that there window come out of a thedral, *also* in Europe."

"Really?" I said.

"Yes, miss. In fac', ebrything we got in the house come out of somewheres."

We were passing a series of elaborate carved linenfold chests and armoires in the upstairs hall. We turned right, and Magothy opened a stout oak door.

"Here yo' is, miss. Now I got to tell the Madam that there doctuh, he back."

I was inside a room that might have come out of a museum, and really ought to have been left in it. A high curtained bed, a prie-dieu with a rushlight on it, a carved oak chest, a carved oak bench in front of a high stone fireplace. The fireplace was a lovely paneled thing, and there was a cheery little blaze behind a pair of fine wrought-iron firedogs. I can't say that even then the place was particularly homey, and there wasn't anything to sit down on that had a cushion on it. And there was certainly nothing inviting about the heavily curtained bed except the steps you had to use to get into it.

However, the bathroom adjoining, with polished rose quartz, inlaid jade and amber water lilies, more than made up for it. By the time I'd had a bath in the delicate aromatic stuff that gushed out of the concealed faucet, I was a new woman.

Aspasia came, a neat mulatto in brown poplin, and put my things away. She said, "Is there anything else, miss?"

I said, "Yes. One thing. Who is Michael Spur?"

She said, "Michael Spur, miss? Is he white or colored?"

He might have been Siamese, for all I knew, so I let the matter drop.

I'd finished dressing when Cheryl Trent tapped at my door and came in, a slim, charming daffodil of a girl in sea green tulle with quaint puffed little sleeves and a long slim skirt flowering out into a billow of ruffles at her gold shod feet. The yellow curls still clustered at the back of her neck, but the rest of her head was set in sleek shining waves, with just a curl escaping here and there to prove she wasn't too sleek and shining.

"Ready?" she asked.

"When I get a handkerchief. Now."

But she had sat down on the bench in front of the fire and was looking at me with two wide-set unsmiling blue eyes.

18

"I didn't mean to be so rude to you this afternoon," she said seriously.

I smiled.

"I wasn't, really. I mean, I was just surprised," she went on. "I didn't expect to see Dr. Sartoris, in the first place, and I didn't know you knew him . . . and, well, I didn't expect you to look like . . . I mean, I thought you'd be about forty, and maybe fat, or awfully thin, and wear glasses, and talk about your work. You know?"

"Yes," I said, "I know."

There wasn't any use telling her I was practically thirty, and that anyway forty wasn't horribly old.

"That's what the women who write things that come to see Mother look like. They all give me a pain in the neck. When Dad said you were coming, and for me to meet you, I thought we were in for it again. Dad said you wouldn't be so bad, because he knew McCrae wouldn't send anybody terribly poisonous down."

She was talking quite as if she were speaking about somebody out in the garden. I gathered there was nothing personal intended, really.

"How long have you known Dr. Sartoris?" she asked abruptly.

"About six hours, roughly, I should say."

She looked at me with a surprised puzzled expression in her eyes.

"Oh!" she said. "I mean, really? I don't mind, you know."

I saw she hadn't understood me.

"I ran into him, literally," I said, "at noon today, outside Mr. McCrae's office. That's the first time I ever laid eyes on him. Then he was on the train coming down, and we introduced ourselves and talked. You know how you do on trains."

As a matter of fact my only other experience of the sort had been with a very young missionary returning from China, and I talked with him from Seattle to New York.

"I've never been in a train alone," she said simply.

"It's fun," I said. "You ought to try it some time."

She nodded.

"Did he tell you anything about us?" she asked, as abruptly as before.

"He said you were all terribly nice, except somebody. I've forgotten just now who it was."

"I guess it was Dad. Or maybe Dick—that's Major Ellicott. Or maybe he meant Mr. Archer, Dad's lawyer?"

"I don't remember," I said.

"Did he tell you about Michael Spur?"

"No, he didn't."

"And you really never knew him before? Not really?"

"Never," I said patiently.

She traced the pattern in the Aubusson rug with her little gold shoe, and bit her under lip thoughtfully.

"Then you wouldn't know, would you," she said, after a moment.

"Know what?"

"Whether he'd know."

It was too confusing for me. I sat down on the bed steps, hoping she'd explain just what she did mean.

"I mean, if you never knew him before, you wouldn't know whether he'd be apt to be right when he says Michael Spur will murder one of us when he comes."

"Good Lord," I said, "what *are* you talking about?"

She looked wide-eyed and surprised.

"Of course," she said; "I forgot. You don't know about Michael, do you?"

"No, I don't."

"Well, you see, he murd——"

There was a tap on the door. She stopped abruptly. I said "Come," and Aspasia looked in.

"Your father is waiting for you-all, miss," she said.

"All right," Cheryl said. She got up. "Let's go. I'll tell you after dinner."

THREE

I was anxious to meet Duncan Trent. There's something romantic and appealing about a man who started life with nothing but determination and a pair of copper-toed boots and amassed a great fortune. I'd thought it was going to be fun to play ghost to such a man. He wasn't too well known; he'd never had a press conference and passed out his views on agriculture, politics or dressmaking in the home. I don't suppose he had any, actually—not that that seems to restrain most self-made millionaires. Anyway, I was definitely interested in the job of visiting his home and writing his autobiography. I didn't know then that the time had already passed too far along for Mr. Duncan Trent's autobiography ever to be written, or that my stay at Ivy Hill was going to be like a Grand Guignol, with midnight screams and murder and staring-eyed Death meeting you almost at every turn.

Half-way down the wide staircase Cheryl, calm as a lily, said suddenly, "I'm glad you came. Don't go right away, will you."

"I was asked for two weeks," I said smiling.

"I know. But you don't know what it's like here, yet. Promise me you'll stay."

We were passing the last of the grotesque hollow iron-and-chain knights on the landing when she said that. Just as I started to say "All right—I promise," the spear fell from his mailed fist and landed on the polished floor in front of us with a sharp clatter. It nearly scared the wits out of both of us.

Cheryl drew her breath sharply, and bent down to pick it up.

"Magothy says when things in a house fall like that it means somebody is going to die."

She was trying to speak lightly, as she stood the spear up in the corner back of the knight, but you could see she was

21

forcing it. And I had a queer icy fluttering inside of me, in spite of myself. I looked up at the darkening rose window, and at the tattered flags hanging limply from the balcony. For a moment there seemed something almost ominous in the air. Then we heard a deep burst of laughter, and the clink of ice on crystal. There's something practical and clear-headed about a cocktail, even if it's just tomato juice.

"It's funny, isn't it," I said, "how contagious superstitions like that are?"

"I guess it is," she said.

We went on down. When we went into the living room five men in dinner dress turned from the business of cocktails to greet us. Before the short plump little man with a white Vandyke beard and practically no hair on his head had crossed the room, I had seen that Dr. Sartoris was there, more impressive than ever in his dinner jacket, and that at the other end of the line there was a tall dark-haired man with a tiny mustache who was just as attractive. I think Dr. Sartoris must have seen my glance skip the short pink-gilled white-haired jovial person, and the little brown-eyed rabbit of a man, between him and the tall dark man who I naturally assumed was Major Ellicott. At least I caught an amused twinkle in his eyes while Cheryl was introducing me to her father.

"Ah, there, Boswell," said Mr. Trent genially, "it's mighty nice to have you down here."

He shook my hand warmly, and looked me over—I felt a little like a horse—and pinched his daughter's smooth cheek affectionately.

"See, Cherry—I told you."

Then he led me across the room towards the great Florentine fireplace where they were standing.

"My Boswell, gentlemen," he said. "You know Dr. Sartoris? If he thinks you're a ghost of any sort, he'll throw you out. Don't like ghosts. You call 'em something else, eh, doctor?"

Dr. Sartoris smiled. It was rather pleasant, some way, having him on my side; and that's exactly the impression his smile, and the little pressure on my fingers as we shook hands, conveyed.

"This is Mr. Archer, Boswell. He'll censor everything we write so we can't be had up for libel. Watch him, Boswell."

Mr. Archer's pink fat cheeks swelled like a Falstaffian sunfish. " 'S a pleasure, Miss Cather," he beamed. "We'll have to get together. Duncan's got too much of a past to let it all out, you know."

He shook with mirth, and the others laughed more or less politely. I didn't make out whether it was funny because Mr. Trent did have a past or didn't.

"And this is my brother-in-law, Perry Bassett," Mr. Trent said. "Don't pick any flowers, and don't walk on the grass—eh, Perry? He'll be after you, Boswell, with a pruning knife. Eh, Perry?"

Perry Bassett—he was always just that, I learned later, never Mr.—looked at me like a dog who hopes you won't kick him, and we shook hands. It was an odd sensation, after the smooth and well cared-for hands of Dr. Sartoris and Mr. Archer. Perry Bassett's hands were like sandpaper.

"I hope you'll pick all the flowers you like, Miss Cather," he said, in a low gentle voice. To this day almost the only things I can remember of Perry Bassett are those rough dirt-soiled hands, the gentle voice, the animal-like look in his brown eyes.

"And this," said Mr. Trent, "is my cousin Major Ellicott. If Cheryl can spare him he'll show you the place—horses, golf, boats, anything."

Major Ellicott bowed. I could quite understand how Cheryl might not be able to spare him, and so could he, I thought. He smiled at me, holding my hand a bare fraction of a second too long. His smile was politely faint and ironic —as if he knew all women found him irresistible.

"I hope you'll like us," he said. There was something in his voice that said he'd be crushed if I didn't like them, especially him, and I could believe it if I wanted to.

I turned back to Mr. Trent and Cheryl, and took the thin-stemmed bubble of glass that Magothy offered me on the silver tray. I was saying how glad we were on the magazine that Mr. Trent had at last consented to let us use his story, which we all felt was so inspiring. Or something like that. Actually I was wondering how the deuce a household managed to get along with two men like Dr. Sartoris and Major Ellicott in it. They were so dreadfully alike, except that one was dark and the other light. I glanced at Cheryl, blonde and cool and lovely.

Mr. Trent was saying, "Yes, Cheryl and Dick here"—he pointed with his glass at Major Ellicott—"are getting married in June, and then I'm taking a cruise around the world."

"Really?" I said, and glanced at Major Ellicott. I don't

know why I should have been so astonished. Cheryl was talking to Dr. Sartoris, her face lifted up, her eyes and lips laughing. He was telling her how I'd nearly knocked him down outside Mr. McCrae's door. He was being sort of gentle and big-brotherly, and all the rest of it. It seemed strange, in some way. I hadn't noticed before that Cheryl was wearing a large diamond solitaire.

I was just thinking, while listening to Mr. Trent, that there were two more people in the household, and wondering vaguely about them, when we heard the sharp click of heavy heels on the stairs, and in a moment a large, well-corseted, henna-haired, heavily made-up woman in a red print dinner gown appeared in the doorway. For an instant she regarded us through her platinum lorgnette. Then she smiled archly.

"Good evening, everybody!" she said brightly.

"Emily, this is Miss Cather," said Mr. Trent.

"Oh," said Mrs. Trent. "Pleased to meet you, I'm sure."

I had actually touched the fat scarlet-tipped bejeweled fingers she extended before she turned and was greeting Dr. Sartoris.

"How sweet of you, doctor!" she said. "I was *so* pleased and *so* surprised when Cheryl said she'd run into you at the station. Were you *really* coming here, to see *us?*"

In view of the telegram I'd illicitly read, that seemed strange. But apparently not to Dr. Sartoris.

He bowed over her hand.

"It is the radio-chemistry of ideas, Mrs. Trent," he said.

She nodded and said simply, "A matter of spiritual tuning-in."

I looked at her quickly in spite of myself, but she wasn't being funny at all.

"What do you make of it, Boswell?" said Mr. Trent. There was an ironic little grin on his face. "You up on that stuff?"

"I'm afraid not, Mr. Trent," I admitted.

Mrs. Trent raised her platinum lorgnette and her plucked brows and looked vaguely around the room. I turned my back on Dr. Sartoris. I couldn't bear to face him after that. It didn't seem decent.

At that point Magothy announced dinner, and we put down our glasses. Mrs. Trent brushed off a couple of bits of caviare and toast that had got becalmed on her plentiful bosom, and handed Dr. Sartoris her glass with a coquettish little flip of the eyebrows. She moved towards the door.

Then there occurred the first sharp rift in what turned out to be an evening full of them.

"Where's Miss Hutton, Emily?" Mr. Trent said curtly.

Mrs. Trent stopped, and turned around, and her rouged lips were set firmly.

"She's got ears, she can hear bells," she said angrily. "If Miss Hutton can't be down in time for dinner, she can go without it."

"We'll wait," said Mr. Trent quietly. "Magothy, go upstairs and tell Miss Hutton dinner is ready."

But Magothy did not have to go. Sharp light steps were coming quickly down the stairs, and a woman with dark sleek hair, parted in the middle and drawn like a silky sheath over a finely modeled head, appeared in the door. Her face was white, with a very red mouth and narrow finely arched brows that made Mrs. Trent's scanty crop look cheap and ridiculous. Agnes Hutton had long drooping lashes. She was exquisite, I thought, in a smooth-fitting gown of coral satin, high at the neck in front and nothing anywhere in back.

"I'm sorry I'm late, Mrs. Trent," she said in a soft purring voice. She gave Mr. Trent a slow half-open smile, and turned to the other men, still more or less lined up against the amazing Renaissance Florentine fireplace that dominated the enormous green and gold living room. One thing seemed clear. Agnes Hutton certainly had not expected to see Dr. Sartoris. Her whole body moved perceptibly under the shock, and her eyes widened just an instant before she caught herself and sunk back behind her slit white mask.

"Good evening, doctor," she said quietly, and when Mr. Trent said, "This is Miss Cather whom I told you about, Agnes," she extended her hand quite cordially and said, "Of course, Mr. Trent. How do you do, Miss Cather. We're ever so anxious for you to begin. You've got a fascinating job. I can't imagine anybody's life that's more interesting or worth while to do."

I remember thinking at the time that it seemed a little thick, but that she probably knew the correct thing to say. Mr. Trent looked perceptibly pleased, Mrs. Trent angry and a little futile, as if she should have thought of something of the sort herself. Major Ellicott raised one eyebrow and smiled ever so slightly. Cheryl's and Dr. Sartoris's eyes met inscrutably, Mr. Archer cleared his throat and frowned a little, Perry Bassett looked a little ashamed. I was a little surprised. It was such bald open-faced flattery, too obvious

25

for a man to swallow, even from his secretary. In public, anyway. Mr. Trent, however, didn't seem to find it difficult. Nor did the fact that that simple remark instantly congealed the last pretense at general cordiality in the room seem to bother him—or not at first.

"I *have* had some interesting experiences," he was saying, as the rest of us followed Mrs. Trent into the dining room in more or less of a constrained silence.

The Trents' dining room was high and darkly paneled—lifted bodily from some Elizabethan manor house in Cornwall, Mrs. Trent told me later. The table, gleaming with silver and lace and slender red tulips, was a candle-lit island in a dark sea, so dark that Magothy and his assistant would have been invisible except for their shirt fronts and their white cotton gloves.

We sat down. I could feel a tense ominous something close in behind me as solidly, almost, and as definitely, as the high back of my chair. I didn't know then that that solid and definite something was Death, or that Death was there behind us, waiting in the deep shadows, his icy finger lifted, ready to point at one, two, three of us. But I did have so real a sense of something there that I turned with a start and looked back over my shoulder. It was only Magothy with my soup. But I wasn't the only one who was uneasy. Mr. Trent's voice had a sharp cutting edge as he pushed back his chair and stood up, tiny beads of perspiration on his high bald forehead.

"For God's sake, Emily, can't we have some light in here?" he demanded angrily. "Magothy, turn on the lights."

Magothy hobbled over to the wall, and the room was flooded with soft overhead light. It wasn't quite as romantic as the dim flickering light from the two seven-branch candelabra, but we all seemed to breathe a little easier.

But before we had got to the broiled young chicken and asparagus, I realized that all the light in the world would not help the situation at that table. There was something distinctly wrong, and they were all trying to cover it up or evade it. All except Mrs. Trent, oddly enough, and Agnes Hutton. Dr. Sartoris and Mr. Archer did their best to hold the conversation away from something—whatever it was—but without success. Perry Bassett suddenly dropped his fork, and Mrs. Trent turned on him with a convulsive start, like a fury.

"*Will* you stop that fidgeting, Perry? You'll drive me crazy!"

26

And then she put down her own fork, and leaned forward with a look of determination. The corners of her mouth were drawn down a little.

"Duncan," she demanded in a high and charged voice, "*when* is Michael Spur coming here?"

There was a moment of dead silence.

Then Mr. Trent looked impatiently at his secretary.

"He didn't say, Mr. Trent," Agnes Hutton said. "His wire read 'Coming back,' and was signed 'Michael Spur,' as I've already told Mrs. Trent a great many times today. It was sent from New York at two-five last night, and it got here at nine-fifteen this morning."

Mr. Trent looked at his wife.

"You know all I know," he said shortly.

Mrs. Trent was making a definite effort to control her voice.

"I think you ought to find out something about him before you let him come here," she said. "It's your duty. He has no right here."

Mr. Trent's face flushed.

"He has every right here, Emily," he said angrily. "His father was my partner and my friend. What money I have, I made because Stephen Spur backed me to the last ditch. Tom Archer and I are co-trustees of Stephen's estate, and we are Michael Spur's guardians."

Mrs. Trent moistened her lips, pale and dry under the thick coating of lipstick.

"But, Duncan!" she cried. "I mean the boy's health! It isn't safe for any of us—there's no telling what may happen! He might murder all of us in our beds!"

"Rubbish!" Mr. Trent said with an angry snort. "Poppycock!"

Heavy purple veins stood out at his temples, and a strawberry birthmark in the center of his forehead, which I hadn't noticed before, burned somberly. And yet, I had the strong impression that he would very much like to be convinced that it was rubbish and poppycock.

Up to now I had only seen Mrs. Trent archly condescending, or irritable and ill at ease. I saw now that under all her manner she had an obstinate vitality. Angry spots mottled her heavily powdered face and spread down her flabby white neck; her eyes blazed and her lips were set in a thin line curving downward at the ends, angry, frightened and determined.

"You say that because you're pig-headed and ignorant!"

27

she cried. "Ask Dr. Sartoris. He'll tell you it isn't poppycock! That's what happens in cases like this!"

Everybody, even Mr. Trent, looked at Dr. Sartoris. He leaned back in his chair with great deliberateness, a wise and thoughtful expression on his handsome face. The shadows cast from overhead, and from the fourteen candles on the table, gave it a strong and rugged quality. It was the face of a man to listen to.

"My dear Mrs. Trent," he said, after a thoughtful pause, "I didn't say quite that. I'm almost sorry now that I said anything at all."

Mrs. Trent was suddenly on the verge of tears, and her anger melted like the snow.

"You don't care what happens!" she said, like a plaintive child.

"No, no, my dear friend—that's unkind of you. All I mean is that I've alarmed you, and I may be wrong. I only spoke of what *may* happen, just to protect you. That's all. Let's forget I mentioned it."

He dismissed the matter with a deprecatory smile. Mr. Trent made an inarticulate sound, and Mr. Archer spoke up curtly.

"Do I understand, Doctor, that because of this other business years ago, you think there's danger of this boy's going off again?"

We turned again to look at Dr. Sartoris, and I stole a glance at the other faces caught round the pool of gleaming silver, lace and candlelight there in the center of the great room. Mr. Trent's gray eyes were narrowed, his face was still heavily flushed, the veins still standing out at his temples; but he was listening. Agnes Hutton, her skillfully rouged lips slightly parted, had not once taken her eyes off the great man next to Mrs. Trent. Perry Bassett was making bread pills and piling them up, like a collection of little gray cannonballs, at the base of a silver dish; but he was watching his sister and Dr. Sartoris. Major Ellicott was looking at Cheryl, with his faintly superior smile. And all of them, of course, had completely forgotten that I existed.

"I can answer that question for you," Dr. Sartoris said at last. "Here we have a case of shell shock. This boy was sent home from France when he was only twenty years old. Outwardly, physically, in good shape; psychically, emotionally that is, all wrong. You have enough tragic evidence of that. Mrs. Trent has told me how he used to get up at night and try to find his gun."

28

Mrs. Trent closed her eyes dramatically.

"Oh, don't you remember, Duncan?" she cried. "That night when we found him looking out of his window? He was leaning out, you could tell he was seeing something down in the gardens; and his face was horrible—his voice was ghastly! He was saying 'There he is! Get him! *Stick* him! Ah . . . he's dead!'"

She was leaning forward urgently, her voice sunk to a whisper, horror on her face. She was an actress—she was seeing what Michael Spur had seen: a man hiding and being found; a naked bayonet; a clean thrust; death.

Mrs. Trent sank back in her chair. The table was silent as the grave. Then she leaned forward quickly.

"Then he'd hunt for his gun," she cried. "Don't you remember, Duncan? And then that terrible night he found it— God knows where! And he went out, and you and his father and Dick went after him. Oh my God, and I was watching from my window! And I saw the spurt of fire in the dark; and Stephen Spur was lying there at your feet, dead, murdered by his own son!"

The tears forced themselves under the mascara'd lashes of her closed eyes, and fell unchecked on her velvet bosom.

Everybody at the table seemed moved, even Major Ellicott, who I thought was probably not often moved by anything.

"I didn't know you remembered it so well, Emily," he said. "You ought to forget it. It's dangerous."

She made a little futile gesture. Mr. Trent his head sunk forward, was staring at some point far away past the candles in front of him. He looked up with a start when Dr. Sartoris began to speak again, which he did with a little of the air, I thought, of not liking to have Mrs. Trent steal his show.

"You had him put under observation then, I understand," he said, his voice very grave and impressive. "After a few months he was discharged. But if he had been completely restored, I feel that he would have come back here and carried on his father's work. Instead, he wanders off for . . . how long has it been?"

"Fourteen years," said Mr. Archer.

Dr. Sartoris shrugged his large shoulders.

"And now, he's coming back. I should feel that his sending a telegram after midnight is evidence that he's still laboring under emotional strain. And what happens is this: the old associations are still here—the house, the gardens, the rooms, the people. And they may set up the old psychosis. There lies the danger."

He looked quietly round the table, and shook his head a little.

"I could tell you a hundred cases; none as terrible as this, but of the same type. But I don't want to alarm you. All I suggest is that you take all possible care to save this young man from a recurrence of that psychosis—for his sake as well as your own."

There was a long and tense silence before Mr. Trent spoke.

"You think he meant to kill his father?"

Dr. Sartoris hesitated.

"If I say yes," he replied, "I want you to understand very clearly what I mean. In the sense that we all have the Œdipus Complex—in varying degrees, depending on our libidinal structure or soul plasm, and our environmental structure, which is the molding of soul plasm—we can say that every father is his son's natural enemy, every mother her daughter's."

I stole a glance at Cheryl. She was staring straight in front of her, her attitude startlingly like Mr. Trent's.

"So that while to all appearances young Spur was devoted to his father, I think we can say that that tragic accident was in truth wish fulfillment, the triumph of the libido. You must understand that Michael Spur would be entirely, the most genuinely, unconscious of this desire to kill his father. In his state there's no doubt that he would have shot anyone in his way that night. But you know we never do anything accidentally—not really. That Michael Spur chose his own father to shoot that night was undoubtedly, in my opinion, the Œdipus Complex. There is in all human conduct some motivating force—unconscious, perhaps, but powerful."

He gave us a deprecatory grave smile, and went back to his dessert.

A little silence was broken again by Mr. Archer.

"It doesn't follow, however, that he's a dangerous madman, and that we're all in danger of our lives?"

If Dr. Sartoris noticed the irony in the lawyer's voice he gave no indication of it.

"Oh, not at all," he said calmly. "As I've assured Mrs. Trent over and again. No, I'm merely suggesting, as a physician and a friend, that Michael Spur's return to the very spot where that terrible thing occurred—to the very spot, still, I understand, unchanged—may cause an emotional throwback.

That in turn would result in a recurrence of the old illness. In which case, I must repeat, unless precautions are taken, there is a definite possibility of a similar tragedy."

Mr. Trent cleared his throat so brusquely that I started.

"I don't know anything about the Œdipus Complex," he said angrily, "and I don't want to. But when you or anybody else, your Dr. Freud included, tells me that Michael Spur wanted to kill his father, because he was jealous of his mother's love, when his mother had been dead for five years —if that's what you mean by your Œdipus Complex, well, it's a damnable outrage!"

His voice rose to a shout, and he brought his fist down on the table with a crash.

The quiver of silver and glass died away in a faint musical blur. Duncan Trent glared savagely at Dr. Sartoris, who sat imperturbably at the other end of the table. For the first time since we had sat down Perry Bassett spoke.

"I suggest, Duncan," he said gently, "that it wouldn't do any harm to let the doctor talk to Michael, when he comes. It's sometimes possible to cure cases of that kind, isn't it?"

Mr. Trent snorted violently. Mr. Archer and Major Ellicott exchanged the sort of masked glances that are usually called "significant."

"I must say I'm glad somebody takes an intelligent attitude about it," Mrs. Trent said, her lips still compressed into a thin red line. "I think Perry is right, Duncan. You ought to persuade Dr. Sartoris to psychoanalyze Michael, and cure him of his Œdipus Complex, so he won't shoot anybody else."

Dr. Sartoris looked a little pained, and I thought he would have preferred a different statement of his procedure. Mr. Trent started to speak; but Mr. Archer, whose habit of blandly ignoring Mrs. Trent must have been long-standing, it was so taken for granted by everybody, including Mrs. Trent, brushed the suggestion aside as if neither Perry Bassett nor his sister had spoken.

"I want to get this straight," he said grimly, in a dry crisp courtroom voice from which all the geniality had gone. "You believe first that on that night here, fourteen years ago, Michael Spur *meant* to shoot and kill his own father. And you believe secondly that when he comes back—tomorrow, tonight, whenever he gets here—there is a definite probability that he will kill someone else, it may be someone at this table, unless he is watched. That is your contention?"

Dr. Sartoris bowed very gravely.

"And I support it," he said, "with many years of experience in treating cases of shell shock and the mental and emotional derangements caused by it."

Mr. Archer's keen blue eyes moved slowly from Dr. Sartoris to Mr. Trent.

"It will take more than that, Duncan," he said, "to make me think there is any harm now in Michael Spur."

Mr. Trent stared moodily down at the table.

Dr. Sartoris' grave face relaxed into a friendly smile.

"Then don't say I didn't give you fair warning," he said. He shrugged lightly, as if perhaps after all the whole thing was not as serious as he'd been pretending. His calm gaze moved slowly down the long table, resting for a diagnosing instant on each of the seven faces. When it came to Mr. Archer's the doctor who was Mrs. Trent's adviser and the lawyer who was Mr. Trent's looked steadily at each other for a long moment. I doubt if many people had ever met Mr. Archer's blue cold stare so unwaveringly.

Mrs. Trent breathed heavily and got to her feet. We all got up except Mr. Trent. He remained seated at the head of the table, staring at some point far beyond the crystal goblet in front of him.

"Well," Mrs. Trent said, with a sort of vague bitterness, and without so much as a glance in his direction, "I hope we aren't murdered in our beds. That's all I can say. It's well enough for you to scoff at things you don't understand. I for one *believe* in psychology."

She sailed out of the room like a large red battleship, her daughter and I following, Agnes Hutton bringing up the rear.

FOUR

The rich heady odor of Mr. Trent's Havanas and the sound of men's voices followed us out across the hall, and died away as the old butler closed the door. Mrs. Trent settled herself fretfully behind the coffee tray in front of the fifteenth century Florentine fireplace. From the determined lines of her mouth I thought we were in for a lecture on psychology. It was logical enough, considering her, and what they had been talking about. I had never seen any of these people, of course, before I'd left New York, but a newspaper woman sees too many Mrs. Trents in the course of a year not to recognize the type at once. If she hadn't believed in psychology she'd have believed in something else, and in another six months she'd have "done" psychology and would be getting around to "doing" the Technocrats—though I doubt if you'd find a Technocrat as good-looking as Dr. Sartoris.

But I was wrong—about Mrs. Trent, not the Technocrats. I was just beginning to learn that Mrs. Trent never talked, when she could help it—not even about psychology—when her husband's secretary was around, unless Dr. Sartoris happened to be there too. She had been so imposing when we left the dining room that it was a shock to see her deflate, as if her confidence in herself and psychology were seeping out of her like air out of a big red balloon.

Agnes Hutton, cool and aloof, sat at one side of the fireplace in a high-backed Jacobean chair, smiling what struck me as an irritatingly superior Mona Lisa smile, her large blue eyes half-veiled under heavily shaded lids. She apparently never spoke, I thought; but when Mrs. Trent put too much coffee in the little gold Lennox cup so that it slopped over, she moved her body ever so slightly, as if she'd had a sudden pain somewhere. She was quite maddening. Personally, I thought, I should have thrown something at her. I imagine Mrs. Trent must have wanted to many times.

33

The odd thing was that she really hardly ever said anything, so that one scarcely had a chance to be rude to her. I think the only time she really disturbed her smile to speak was when, just after she had murmured "No sugar, please, Mrs. Trent," Mrs. Trent, vapid and preoccupied, promptly dropped two lumps in the small cup. Agnes Hutton's delicately arched brows raised, and the smile deepened at one corner of her mouth. She turned a little toward me.

"That's psychology, isn't it?" she said. "Dr. Sartoris would say Mrs. Trent really wanted me to get fat."

Cheryl Trent, who had been restlessly fiddling with the radio at the other end of the room, caught her lower lip between her teeth and gave the dial an angry twist that filled the room with a savage blast of sound. She turned it down again and sauntered over to her mother.

"We don't have to worry about our figures, do we, darling?" she said, kissing her lightly on the top of the head. "It's a gorgeous night, Miss Cather. Let's go outside."

"All right," I said.

Mrs. Trent hastily put down her coffee cup and pushed back the tray. It was plain that she had no intention of being left alone with Agnes Hutton. Miss Hutton watched her coolly with that maddening smile. As Cheryl and I stepped through the long window onto the tiled terrace, we heard Mrs. Trent's high sharp heels strike the uncarpeted hardwood floor of the hall.

Outside I took a deep breath. It was like a sharp sudden relief from pain to get out of that house into the cool sane night. In front of us stretched a long moon-drenched garden; at the end of it, between two tall perfectly matched poplars, lay the Ivy Hill bay, and out beyond the Chesapeake. On both sides of the garden was a high thick wall of closely clipped box. Its faintly exotic perfume was lost in the warm odor of the great crescent-shaped bed of blue and red and pink and white tulips just beyond the low terrace that led down to the long garden.

Cheryl, standing beside me, pointed to the white marble bench gleaming faintly in the moonlight a little way down.

"That's where it happened," she said quietly. "The blood stain is still on the bench. Mother was upstairs. She'd wanted Michael sent away to a sanatorium, and his father and Dad and Major Ellicott were in the library talking with Dr. O'Brien from Annapolis about it. He was shellshocked, and did all sorts of funny things, but only at night when he was supposed to be asleep."

She hesitated. Then she said, "I've never told Mother this. One night I was supposed to be asleep, but I sneaked downstairs to get a bar of chocolate Major Ellicott had given me. I'd hid it from the governess—I was only six, you see. It was dark, but I got the bar, and I was going back upstairs when I saw somebody on the landing. I was scared stiff. I got behind one of Mother's chairs in the hall and hid. I was dreadfully frightened. It was Michael. He came down the stairs and stood looking up at Mother's rose window, his eyes wide open and staring and wild. He kept saying something like 'They've taken my gun, but I'll get him.' His voice was horrible. Then all of a sudden he reached out and took the spear out of the knight's hand, and crept on down the stairs. He was coming straight at me. I could see him because it was bright moonlight, just like tonight. And I had on white pajamas, so he could see me too. He got closer and closer, and the spear raised in his hand, and I knew he was going to kill me, but I couldn't scream or do anything. I just waited. And I saw his arms go back—he had it in both hands, like a bayonet—and the spear came slowly at me; and then suddenly his arms relaxed and he dropped the spear on the rug. Then he rubbed his hand over his eyes and pushed back his hair, the way he always did, and he knelt down beside me and picked me up in his arms and held me tight. He said 'Cherry, honey, I'm sorry, did I scare you?' He was so sweet, and I said, 'No, Mikey.' He said 'I'll take you upstairs. Will you forgive me, Cherry?' and I said I would. Next day I got spanked for getting chocolate all over my pajamas, but I never told on him. And it was the next night he shot his father. Then they took him away."

Inside someone had turned the radio on. Outside the only sound was the croaking of the frogs in the distance.

"But you see, don't you?" Cheryl asked.

"See what?" I said.

"I mean, he must have *wanted* to kill his father, or he would have stopped before he did it. The way he did with me that night. I didn't tell Dr. Sartoris, but I sort of made up a case, and he said that such a person would always stop before he did anything he didn't really will to do. He said nobody could make a hypnotized person do anything against his own deep-grained convictions. I mean you can't hypnotize a person and make him commit murder unless he really wants to do it."

"Listen, Cheryl," I said. "Don't you see what's happened to all you people? You've been thinking about this thing till you've all got the jitters. You forget that Michael Spur has been away fourteen years. He's probably cured, in the first place. And even if he isn't, and even if he wanted to kill his father, you don't suppose he's going to want to kill everybody else here, do you?"

She shook her head reluctantly.

"He'll probably walk in a successful bond salesman, or something, and you'll all be ashamed of yourselves for letting a . . ."

I started to say "a charlatan" but changed it quickly.

". . . for letting Dr. Sartoris get you in this state."

"It isn't only Sartoris. It's Agnes Hutton too."

"What's she got to do with it?"

"Michael used to be engaged to her. Oh, that's not really it, but you know how you get worried about things."

I started to say something more when suddenly her hand closed tightly on my arm. I looked at her quickly. She was staring down the garden, her eyes wide, her breath coming in quick short gasps. I followed her eyes.

A tall dark figure was moving out of the deep shadow of the box, slowly, like a man in pain. His head was bare. He came forward with slow heavy steps until he stood by the marble bench. I saw him raise his hand to his head and brush back his hair like a man in a dream. Suddenly he knelt down and touched the bench.

We stood there breathless, watching him. There was a noise behind us. I looked back. It was Agnes Hutton. She was looking down there too, a lighted cigarette arrested midway to her lips. I felt Cheryl's body stiffen. Miss Hutton looked at her; her cigarette completed the graceful arc to her mouth. She took a deep puff, exhaled it slowly, then, with her maddening smile flicked the cigarette into the tulip bed. She turned without a word and went back into the house.

"God, how I hate that woman," Cheryl whispered savagely.

"Let's go in," I said. She held my arm.

"Wait," she whispered. I looked back down the garden.

Michael Spur had risen, and was coming toward us, slowly. On the other side of the flower bed he looked up, and saw us standing there. Between us the thin blue line of smoke from Agnes Hutton's cigarette coiled into the air.

Michael Spur reached down and picked it up.

"Perry doesn't like cigarette butts in the flower beds, Cherry," he said with a smile. "Hello!"

"Hello, Michael!"

He came round the tulips and looked down at her.

"You've grown up, haven't you, Cherry."

She nodded. A tear caught in her long silky lashes, glistened a moment there, and fell.

"Yes," she said. "Didn't you know?"

"Yes, I knew. That's why I came back."

Cheryl Trent caught her breath in something like a little sob.

"Michael—this is Louise Cather."

"Hello, Louise," he said, with a grin.

"Hello, Michael," I said, and we shook hands.

FIVE

I didn't go inside with Cheryl and Michael Spur. Somehow the atmosphere in there was too overcharged for comfort. But I couldn't help hearing Mrs. Trent's stifled scream just as the window closed and blotted out everything but the croaking frogs and the lapping waves on the shore. And because I didn't want to just stand there, I wandered along the path in front of the house until I came to a stone bench under a lilac bush, sat down, closed my eyes and listened to the odd night noises. I shivered involuntarily, and found myself wishing for the reassuring rattle and dash of the Third Avenue L. I think I was rather frightened. So I said to myself, "My girl, this will never do." I got a cigarette out of my case, but I didn't have a match. I just sat there, trying to make up my mind that this wasn't a madhouse and that everything would be swell in the morning.

I had almost convinced myself of it when I heard a voice not far from me. It was Agnes Hutton. She was behind the lilac bush, so that I couldn't see her. I realized also that my dress, one of those lace things with a tricky jacket you can pack and unpack and wear most any time, was dark, and that she couldn't see me. I was about to speak to let her know I was there; but I heard her soft husky voice saying "If she's half as smart as she thinks she is, you've got to be careful. Swell time to have a stranger here. No . . . no . . . please; stop it! Don't make love to me. That's not the point. Anyway, we'd better go in."

I heard a subdued male voice, but although by this time I was listening as hard as I could, I couldn't catch what he was saying or who he was. I sat perfectly still until they'd gone. Then I got up and slipped quickly back along the grass and through the long window into the living room.

It was empty, and I sat down quietly in a corner of the sofa in front of the fireplace and picked up a magazine. Just then I heard someone behind me.

"Oh, here you are."

It was Agnes Hutton. I looked around. She was standing in the door, smiling.

"I've been looking everywhere for you. Cheryl said you were outside."

I smiled at the absurdity of such an idea.

"Have you been here long?"

"Not very. Why?"

"Mr. Trent wants to see you. I told him you were probably frightfully tired and didn't want to listen to anything tonight. Not even *his* childhood."

"I'm not really tired at all," I said. "If he's not . . . too busy."

"You mean about Michael Spur? That's all Mrs. Trent's nonsense. Don't let it worry you. Mr. Trent doesn't, you know. He's used to it."

"To what?"

I wondered if Michael Spur or some similar person returned every week or so.

"Oh, I mean to Mrs. Trent's fads and fears. This psychology is just the latest. A little over a year ago she turned nudist and made poor Perry Bassett go round the place in shorts and a pair of sandals. It was very funny, because Perry insisted on wearing his old brown hat too. Then the high priest of the cult ran off with her French maid, so it didn't last. Then she met Dr. Sartoris at a tea in Baltimore, and took up psychology. Oh, it's a great place," she added with a delicately stifled yawn. "Never a dull moment. You won't forget to drop in the library to see Mr. Trent before you go to bed? They're all having a powwow in there now. Good night."

I must have looked a little surprised. After all, it wasn't ten o'clock yet. She laughed a soft gurgling little laugh that was rather attractive, mostly because it didn't sound at all like her silky Mona Lisa smile.

"Yes—I'm getting out of the way," she said. "You'll always find it best when there's a family conclave. Always ends in a frightful row."

She was quite right. It wasn't five minutes before I heard a door slam violently and Mrs. Trent came storming across the hall into the living room, almost beside herself. Her brother and Dr. Sartoris were following her. I didn't quite get what had happened. I learned later that Mr. Trent had ordered Dr. Sartoris out of the house and Mrs. Trent had threatened to go with him, and Mr. Trent had told her to go ahead and good riddance.

"He wants to get me out of here so he can have that woman in my place," she cried hysterically. "I'll never go now. I'll just show him!"

"Now, my dear Emily," said Dr. Sartoris firmly. "You're not quite yourself. Sit down and be calm a moment—do you hear me?"

I'd got out by that time.

The library door was ajar. I pushed it open and stepped inside. It was a high paneled room lined with mellow old calf volumes that looked as if nothing had disturbed a single one of them for centuries.

Mr. Trent and his lawyer Mr. Archer and Michael Spur were sitting around the large table, talking earnestly. I backed out, but Mr. Trent caught sight of me.

"Come in, Miss Cather," he said, getting up with a smile. "Have you met Michael Spur?"

"Yes, we've met."

"That's fine. Well, Archer, we'll look into the business tomorrow. I want to talk to my Boswell a while and just get our bearings."

Mr. Archer smiled genially, and he and Michael Spur got up.

"What about a rubber of bridge, Michael?" he said. "How's your game?"

"Just fair, sir."

"Fine. Just what I like."

"Be careful of him, Michael," said Mr. Trent. "He'll get your shirt."

"That's about all I've got, sir," Michael Spur grinned.

I was almost startled to see the change that had come over Mr. Trent. His face was tired and drawn, and he sat down heavily when the two of them had gone, as if the business of keeping up a genial front had suddenly got to be too much for him.

"Well, that's that," he said. "Sit down over here, Miss Cather. I want to talk to you."

I took the chair Michael Spur had been sitting in and faced him across the table. There was an amber-silk-shaded lamp between us. He pushed it aside and leaned forward, his hands folded in front of him.

"Have you ever thought what a shingle that's caught in an eddy in the tide feels like?" he said. I shook my head.

"Well, that's just what I feel like," he went on. "My ideas

about this autobiography of mine have changed a good deal since McCrae first talked to me about it."

"You don't mean we're not going to write it?"

He laughed what the old melodrama called a mirthless laugh. I felt distinctly not at ease.

"Yes, we're going to write it," he said. "But it's going to be different."

He seemed lost in thought for a moment. Then he said, "But that can wait"—as it turned out, a profoundly and tragically untrue statement. "There's something else I want to talk to you about first. Cheryl says you know this fellow Sartoris. What kind of a bird is he?"

"Cheryl's wrong, Mr. Trent," I said. "I don't know him at all. I met him today for the first time."

"That straight?" he demanded quickly. Through the thick lenses of his horn-rimmed spectacles his eyes stared coldly at me.

"That's straight, Mr. Trent," I replied.

"Then he's not a famous New York doctor?"

"He may be. I just don't happen to have heard of him."

I suppose I might have told him that Dr. Sartoris had been in our office to see McCrae that morning, but I didn't. It's always hard to know what to tell people and what not to. I usually manage to do just the wrong thing.

"Well," he said abruptly, "what do you think of this nonsense about young Spur?"

"You mean that he may kill someone else because he killed his father here?"

He nodded impatiently.

"I should think any doctor would agree that it's perfectly possible, Mr. Trent," I said. "But I don't know much about it."

He grunted.

"You think I did wrong in telling that fellow to get out of here and mind his own business? You think maybe the boy is still dangerous? I'm running into trouble by not letting Sartoris take him in hand?"

"I don't know, Mr. Trent, really," I protested feebly. "I don't think Dr. Sartoris would hurt him."

His manner changed instantly.

"That's where you're wrong," he said quickly. "That's just where you're wrong. You don't know anything about it. There's something wrong about that fellow. And that's another thing I want to ask you about. If it was just my wife I wouldn't care what he did—but it's my daughter."

He got up and began to pace back and forth along the table. He had just begun to speak again when there was a tap at the door and Michael Spur came in.

It was the first time that I'd got a very clear sight of him. As he stood just inside the door, looking at Mr. Trent for a moment and shaking his head a little, with a queer and despondent look on his face, I saw a tall and almost rugged young man, his face a healthy bronze, his crisp curly hair a chestnut brown that looked as if it had been burned under a tropical sun. His mouth was full and generous, and while he wasn't handsome in the smooth, suave manner of Dr. Sartoris or Cheryl's fiancé Major Ellicott, he was decent and clean-looking and dependable. But the most striking thing about him was his eyes. They were dark, and somewhere in the depths of them there were brooding unhappy shadows that came to the surface whenever his face was in repose. They were apparent now as he came up to the table and sat down.

"Well," he said with a short laugh, "I can't stay in there. I guess it's no use."

He ran his hand through his hair in a gesture of unhappiness and almost of despair.

Mr. Trent cast me a sharp glance.

"I thought I was over all that. I thought I could come back here and take things up, without any trouble. But my God, the place hasn't changed at all. Perry's still bidding a slam on two aces, Aunt Emily's passing, Mr. Archer's doubling. It seems just as though, if I looked up, Dad would be standing there in the door telling Perry to learn how to count."

He sank his head in his hands suddenly, a dry painful sob racking his strong lean body.

"Oh God," he said, "I can't forget it. I killed him! It's just as if it was yesterday."

The glance Mr. Trent gave me was very grave, but his voice was confident.

"Now, my boy," he said gently. "You've got to snap out of it. We can't go on like this. That's all over——"

"I know. It can't go on. That's the worst of it. I figured that out years ago. I forced myself to quit thinking about it. It got to be like a bad dream that really never happened. That's why I came back—I thought I was all over it, and I'd prove it and carry on. But it's no go. I guess I'd better get back to the sticks."

It was at that point that Mr. Trent made what I suppose

was one of the greatest concessions he had ever made in his life.

"Look here, Michael," he said. "Why don't you talk things over with this doctor of Emily's? They say he's very successful with cases like yours. No harm in giving him a try. What's he called himself?—a psychoanalyst."

Michael shook his head.

"No use," he said wearily. "I've been to a couple of 'em. One in San Francisco told me to come back here and one in Chicago told me to stay away. They talk a lot and that's all there is to it. I guess the Chicago one was right. Anyway, I'll clear out in the morning."

Mr. Trent hesitated.

"Well," he said, "we'll talk about it in the morning, anyway. You'd better get to bed."

Talking things over in the morning seemed to be Mr. Trent's approach to all his problems. He put an arm around Michael's shoulders and walked out into the hall with him.

He came slowly back into the library, his head sunk forward on his chest, his hands clasped behind his back, and stood in front of the fireplace, making odd noises in his throat. Then he looked up suddenly with a very odd expression on his face.

"Did it ever occur to you tonight, young lady, that you've sort of stumbled into a pretty funny situation?"

I must have looked puzzled in the extreme, for he laughed shortly.

"Did you ever happen to think, this last hour or so, what a weapon anybody round here has got, if he happens to know how to stir Michael Spur up just right?"

I suppose I did see what he meant, but the expression on my face must still have been rather queer. He laughed again.

"You probably don't know anybody you'd like murdered, young woman," he said. As a matter of fact I could think of several people, just offhand. But I said "No."

He nodded almost absent-mindedly, as if he were thinking very hard about something else.

"Well, there's a couple around here that I could be rid of without losing sleep," he went on. "If that boy does shoot anybody, I hope he's careful who he picks out."

He lapsed into a moody silence again.

"It's funny, now," he said, "his deciding to come back here just now. It's damned funny. Well, Boswell—I'll look into that in the morning. See you about ten. O.K.?"

I nodded and said "Good night, Mr. Trent," and started for the door. He stopped me.

"Look here, young lady," he said earnestly. "Keep an eye on my little girl for me—will you? She means a lot to me."

I smiled. "I'll be glad to, Mr. Trent," I said. "Good night."

I went back into the living room to say good night to Mrs. Trent. She and Dr. Sartoris were playing bridge with Perry Bassett and Cheryl. Mr. Archer and Major Ellicott were engrossed in a game of chess, and Agnes Hutton was sitting in front of the fireplace reading.

When I came in Cheryl looked up and smiled, and her mother said, "Oh, is that you, Miss Mather? We looked all over for you to make a fourth at bridge, but we couldn't find you. So poor Miss Hutton had to read a book."

"I really don't find that a hardship, Mrs. Trent," Agnes Hutton said sweetly. Mrs. Trent flushed. As I had no idea that what she would say, if anything, would help, I broke in. "I'm sorry," I said. "I've been talking to Mr. Trent. Anyway, I'm rather tired, if you'll excuse me."

"That's all right," she said. "You can play tomorrow night. That's my trick. It was my jack."

"I know, mother," Cheryl said patiently. "But Perry trumped it with the two of diamonds. Anyway, mother, Miss Cather's waiting to say good night."

"Oh, good night, Miss Mather."

Mrs. Trent looked around and smiled brightly.

"I hope you get some sleep. Queen Elizabeth slept in your bed. They say it's well over a hundred years old."

SIX

I didn't know as much about the geography of the Trents' house then as I do now, after all that happened there. But I did know that after I got up the wide staircase, past the knights, I had to turn out of the big dimly lighted hall, with the balcony overlooking the foyer downstairs, into a corridor that was still longer and dimmer and even more spacious. My door was the third on the right. I hurried past the oak highboys and the carved chests, very glad to close the heavy door behind me and be alone.

I've wondered a number of times since then whether the course of Queen Elizabeth's long reign would have been a little smoother if she'd had a different bed. It was an enormous bed, heavily carved, with heavy tapestry curtains drawn closely round the head; and it was harder than I'd thought it possible for a bed to be. When I got into it I was very sleepy. After I'd turned off my light, and lay there looking up at the dark curtains all around, I was as wide awake as I'd ever been in my life. At first I thought the bed was entirely responsible. Then I realized that it wasn't. The chief thing I missed was the familiar sound of the L-trains and the honking taxis. I closed my eyes and listened. All I could hear was the loud croaking of the frogs, and when that stopped, in one of those concerted silences, I could hear the far-off lapping of the waves on the beach, and all the tiny unfamiliar country sounds that the frogs drowned out the minute they began to croak again.

I lay there trying to get my city tempo down to the point of sleep, and I got to thinking about the people downstairs, and wondering whether Michael Spur was really dangerous. Or was it just special pleading on Dr. Sartoris's part? After all, I thought, he'd never seen Michael before. He'd probably got everything he knew from Mrs. Trent, and she was certainly both a very prejudiced and a very foolish informant. Then I began to wonder if maybe it wasn't Dr. Sartoris's influence that had convinced Mrs. Trent. Then what Mr. Trent had said came into my thoughts with a rush: Michael's illness could be a powerful weapon in the hands of somebody who could control him.

It all seemed so unusual and complicated. Violent death, or the idea of it, seemed so familiar to all these people, like something they lived with daily, not something remote and horrible. I put the whole matter out of my head, and tried to think about Duncan Trent and how I'd begin a story about him. That wasn't successful, since he'd already warned me that this was going to be a new kind of success story. At last I tried to count sheep jumping over a fence; but after a bit the sheep began to smile a Mona Lisa smile. When the larger ones turned into bundles of red velvet fretfully bleating something about psychology, I sat up and turned on the light.

I reached for one of the two thin white books lying on my bedside table. I'd noticed them before I went down to dinner, observed that they didn't look very exciting, and thought of getting something in the library. But I hadn't done it. The one I now took up was bound in vellum, and was inscribed on the fly-leaf, in a fine flowing hand, "To the future and Emily Trent." The title-page was printed in gold in Old English type. It read "*A Way of Life. An Experiment.* By Victor Paul Sartoris, M.D., Ph.D. Privately Printed."

I thought it would at least have something to tell me about Dr. Sartoris, and settled down to have a look at it. I was wrong. When I'd got halfway through, not having understood a single paragraph, I came to this line: "The erotic-narcissistic-compulsive is therefore, friends and, fellow-seekers, the ideal harmonology of the libido." That finished me. I closed the book and put it respectfully down, thinking I could almost see Agnes Hutton's smile.

The second book was as bad. It was called *A Way of Love*, and apparently was not an experiment, for it was only inscribed "To Mrs. Trent," and seemed to have nothing to say about the future or the past.

After that I tried to go to sleep again, and when that failed I got up. I thought I'd write a letter to Mr. McCrae about Dr. Sartoris, and tell him also about Perry Bassett, since Mr. McCrae grows smilax in a box in his office window over the radiator. I poked up the fire and settled down with a piece of Mrs. Trent's very expensive stationery. But it was no go. My fountain pen was dry, and I knew before I looked that the dish of shot with the quill in it on the prie-dieu had never had any ink in it.

I looked at my watch. It was just twelve o'clock. I didn't of course know what time the Trents went to bed, or whether I could risk going downstairs after some ink, or a book if I could find one. They probably had reading books somewhere; the ones in the library were obviously just decoration. Then I thought of the magazine on the sofa in the living room. I might get hold of it until I could manage something better in the morning.

So I got up, and looked out of the long leaded window. My room was near the center of the long vista to the shimmering bay. The seat where Michael Spur had knelt, the spot where his father had fallen, was white and ghostly, almost phosphorescent in the moonlight. I leaned out. There were no paths of light across the lawn from the open windows downstairs, and I decided I could risk it. I put on my dressing gown and slipped out into the hall. It was absolutely dark. Apparently when the Trents went to bed they believed in turning out the lights.

However, I knew that if I kept in the middle of the hall, and made my way carefully, I could probably get downstairs without knocking over a knight. If I hit a chest or a chair or a highboy it was just my hard luck, but the knights were concentrated on the landing. There were two windows in this end of the hall, and there would be a little light from the rose window. I decided to risk it.

Ordinarily it would have been simple to turn on a light; but I had no notion where or how you did it. The switches were all carefully concealed behind old pieces of tapestry, or under chair rails, and it was pretty confusing until you got the hang of it.

So I went on in the dark. I got to the balcony without bumping into anything. There was light enough from the rose window for me to make out the glint of polished steel, and then the figures of all three knights, standing like ghostly sentinels on the landing. I stood looking down into the hall below; and I became aware then that I had a curious feeling, a sort of uneasiness, vague and indefinable, that something was wrong. And because I haven't any sympathy for vagueness of any sort I promptly put that sensation down to pure funk, brought on by the dark eeriness of a misplaced cathedral window and various skeletons in armor, and proceeded quietly but firmly down the stairs after my magazine.

Just at that point, I'll admit, I should have been glad to have fled back to my room; but it had got to be a point of honor not to let myself be scared out by anything as immaterial as gray shadows.

On the bottom step I came to an abrupt halt.

Someone was still in the library. The door was closed, but there was a faint dim edge of light along the floor, and I could hear someone speaking. At least, I heard a sort of mumbling. I didn't want to get caught prowling around at that hour, and I think I should have gone back then, except that I was wider awake than ever and the living room door wasn't more than twenty feet away. Furthermore, it was open. I decided to make a dash for it, get my magazine and slip upstairs before anybody came out. But it wasn't that easy. I don't mean that anyone came out—at least no one came out into the hall.

I got inside the living room. The heavy gold curtains had been drawn aside, and the moonlight lay in long barred panels across the room. In the instant that I stood there, looking down, a tall dark shadow moved into the white oblong, and fell across my feet, and the shadow of a man's head was blocked against the hem of my nightdress. I looked up, frozen with terror.

A man was standing motionless in the window. For a moment I thought he was inside the room. Then he moved, and I realized that he was outside, and that he did not know that I was behind him, inside the room. I crouched down instinctively, I suppose, behind a chair and waited.

In a minute or two I peered out again. He was still standing there, his back to the window, looking down towards the water. He raised his left hand, and slowly, almost painfully, ran his fingers from his forehead through his hair to the nape of his neck.

I drew a long breath of relief and got up. I didn't mind Michael Spur—which, I suppose, was a tacit admission that I did mind somebody else. Although I don't know just who I thought it was out there. I realized too that the reason I hadn't recognized him was that the moonlight and shadows played tricks with his bulk, so that he seemed thicker than he was.

He didn't look around, and when I reached over the back of the sofa and found somebody had been ahead of me and

48

the magazine was gone, he was still there. There were a couple of decks of cards on the table. I turned to get one of them, and as I did so the shadow on the floor disappeared; Michael Spur had gone as silently as he had come. I put the pack of cards in my pocket and got out of the room.

On the bottom step I hesitated. I could still hear the rumbling sound of voices in the library, and for a moment I thought of looking in and telling Mr. Trent or whoever was there that Michael Spur was out in the garden. But I didn't. I can't help even now, when it's all over, wondering what difference it would have made to everybody—especially to Michael Spur—if I had.

Back upstairs in my room I closed the door and locked it. Then I stood there, wondering if I really ought not to do something about Michael. I decided at last that it was absolutely none of my business, and I'd better go to bed. So I took the stiff red morocco desk pad off the prie-dieu, got into bed, with the help of a pillow on my lap made myself an adequate card table, and dealt out the set-up for a game of patience. Just how long I played I don't know. I heard the muffled but distinct report of the gunshot just as I'd figured out that by Monte Carlo standards I'd lost about $105, had laid down the first seven cards for a new game, and was in the middle of the row of six.

The report was followed by a moment's dull reverberation, and then, instantly, all sounds stopped, even the frogs' croaking, and there was a complete and profound silence.

I sat there motionless, hardly breathing, expecting to hear people rushing around in the hall. There was no sound. I glanced at my watch. It was just two o'clock. I pushed my card table aside and slipped out of bed. It was incredible that no one else in the house should have heard what I had heard. I put on my slippers and dressing gown, unlocked my door and peered out into the hall. The corridor was dark; no one was in it. I listened. There was no sound except for the quick merry note of a clock somewhere striking two.

Then abruptly, almost as if they were reassuring me, the frogs started their loud chorus again.

My first impulse had been to wake someone and tell him I'd heard a shot; but standing there in the dark it flashed across my mind that I'd better be sure before I did anything.

For some reason, I wasn't frightened at all. The blind flash of terror I'd had when Michael's shadow fell across my feet downstairs was gone. In fact, I distinctly remember having a

49

sort of pious sense of being very firm and resolute; and that held up until I got to the balcony and looked down in the eerie grayish light from the rose window. The motionless figures on the landing seemed to have grown suddenly more shadowy and sinister. The long black shadows downstairs seemed to shield moving forms. I felt my heart shrinking, and I looked back to where the shaded light from my bedside threw a dim bar across the black channel of the hall.

I clenched my teeth, assured myself it was too late to turn back, and went downstairs, holding tightly to the banister, and listening for any sound in the gray overwhelming silence. The light in the library was still on; I could see the faint glow under the door; and I ran to it, seized the knob, turned it, and threw the door open with a great wave of relief. "Oh, Mr. Trent!" I gasped.

He was sitting there at the table, just where I had left him, with a pile of papers in front of him. But he did not look up, and I stopped short.

Something stark and primitive laid an icy hand on my heart and drained all power of movement out of my body. It wasn't Mr. Trent who was sitting there at the table—it was death. Death with a head sagging forward, and hand stretched out in front of him, and creeping blood dyeing the starched white bosom of his shirt a living red—like the blossom of the Judas Tree in the waxen banks of the dogwood.

It seemed to me that the pulse of time stopped while I stood there and only the creeping blood moved and swelled. It seemed an eternity, then, but it couldn't have been more than ten or fifteen seconds that I stared, speechless, horribly fascinated, at his sagging head, the gaping wound in his breast, his arms and hands flung out on the table, the papers around them, and the small blueblack revolver lying there among the papers. It was the sight of it that brought me to life. I stepped forward.

And just as I did there was a sharp click, and the library was plunged into total darkness.

For one instant the hard bright image of that terrible scene in front of me stayed in my vision, and even now I can close my eyes and see it—Mr. Trent, the papers, the gun. If only I could have screamed, someone might have come. But I've never screamed in my life. I ran blindly across the room and out into the other hall, and then blundered upstairs, and called, panic-stricken, desperate.

Oddly enough, it was Dr. Sartoris I called. Even odder than that, it was Agnes Hutton who appeared first out of the door next to mine. Then other doors opened, until the dark channel had five more bars of light across it. Perry Bassett, Major Ellicott, Dr. Sartoris, Agnes Hutton and Michael Spur were all out there.

SEVEN

I told them what had happened.

What I remember most clearly now is the abrupt hushed silence, and the way every head turned to Michael Spur as if he'd been a magnet and they were bits of iron. He looked blankly at me, and then at Major Ellicott, standing next to him. Then the color drained from his face and neck, and he raised his left hand to his forehead, and slowly, like a man in a dream, ran his trembling fingers through his curly tousled hair to the nape of his neck.

"My God!" he whispered, and swayed for a second, dazed.

Major Ellicott caught him firmly by the shoulder.

"Brace up, old man," he said sharply. "Get back in your room and stay there, will you, until Doyle gets out here. Agnes, wake Archer and send him downstairs."

I was left standing there, thinking in spite of everything that it was odd that nobody seemed to think of Cheryl and her mother. Then I heard a door open somewhere behind me, and I turned quickly. Cheryl had turned on the light in the transverse hall at the end of the one in which I was standing. She came sleepily toward me.

"What's the matter, Louise?"

My face must have frightened her. Her blue eyes suddenly widened, her lips parted breathlessly.

"There's been an accident, Cheryl," I said gently. "Your father."

"He's dead?" she gasped.

She clutched my arm tightly.

"Yes, Cheryl."

She closed her eyes as if to break the force of the shock. I thought for a moment that she was going to faint, but she didn't. Her grip on my arm tightened, and she leaned forward, every nerve in her body tragically and intensely alive.

"Where is he?" she said.

"In the library."

"I've got to go down."

I caught her arm.

"No," I said. "You don't want to go down. It's rather bad."

"I've *got* to, Louise! You don't understand. They don't care what happens to him!"

"Cheryl dear!" I said as gently as I could, to make her understand. "It's too late. There's nothing you can do. Nobody can do anything for him."

"They can hang him!" she cried passionately. She tore away from me and ran wildly down the hall.

For the first time I understood that it wasn't her father she was talking about. It was Michael Spur.

One thing stands out in my mind in the confusion that followed in the next few hours. That was the tacit agreement, not expressed in so many words by anybody but Cheryl, but perfectly definite nevertheless, that the murder of Mr. Trent was not his tragedy. The tragedy was Michael Spur's. Duncan Trent was an accident. Any one of us might have been sitting there with a bullet through his heart, staring into eternity. It had simply happened to Mr. Trent, and not someone else, and that was all. "A prawn in the hands of fate," Mrs. Trent had called him, with a certain tragic triumph. "I told him so," she said. "You can't get away from psychology. He should have listened to Victor."

It was curious how quickly she dropped any pretense of being on purely formal terms with Dr. Sartoris. She gave the impression of simply turning over her problems to him as if anything that was hers was his too—even a murdered husband. And I must say he rose to the occasion with exactly the sympathetic impressiveness I expected of him. It seemed to annoy Mr. Archer, but he'd been annoyed from the beginning. First at being got out of bed at two o'clock (Perry Bassett whispered to me that he hated having his rest broken, he was most particular about it), and second at Mrs. Trent for keeping everyone waiting, once he was up.

It did take her a very long time to come down. The long streak of mud under her ear, where she hadn't got quite all her complexion pack washed off, was excuse enough for anyone's being slow. There was no particular reason for Mr. Archer to object to her pastel rainbow-hued marabou and peach lace and satin negligee, or to the elaborate and artfully tousled curls over her ear. Except, of course, that it was all rather silly and heartless.

Mr. Archer had no more than time to call her a wicked old woman when Mr. Doyle, the State's Attorney from Annapolis, showed up with Dr. O'Brien. Dr. O'Brien was the coroner, and he was very short and very fat, with a definitely pre-Volstead nose, and generally rather jowly and purple. He wheezed when he talked, and he smoked perfectly foul cigars, which he parked around on mantels and tables so they were always getting knocked off. However, he turned out to be unexpectedly kind-hearted and even sweet about everything, and I don't know how we'd have managed without him.

"You see cases like this cropping up all the time," he said in a whiskey bass, putting down his bag and parking his cigar and shaking hands with Major Ellicott. Both he and Dr. Doyle seemed to know Michael Spur, and to know he was home, and that he'd "gone off again," as Mr. Doyle put it. "Had one last year," Dr. O'Brien went on. "Fella used a hatchet, blood all over the kitchen."

He looked at me, shook his head, and cleared his throat.

"I never get used to it. Always makes me nauseated. Once I was in Venezuela . . ."

"All right, Mr. Archer, we'll look into it," said Mr. Doyle briskly. "You can count on us."

He had been talking with Mr. Archer in low tones in the doorway.

"Ready, Joe?"

Dr. O'Brien picked up his bag and went out into the hall. Major Ellicott followed him, and left me and Agnes Hutton alone. Dr. Sartoris and Mrs. Trent were upstairs with Cheryl and Perry Bassett. Michael, as far as I knew, was still alone in his room.

I glanced over at Agnes Hutton. She was resting her head against the high carved back of a chair with a red velvet seat and gold tassels, staring abstractedly up at the oak-beamed ceiling. She was rather pale, I thought, and her lower lip was caught when I looked at her under the sharp white edge of her teeth. She was a curious contrast to Mrs. Trent. She had on a green flannel tailored dressing gown, her hair was neatly brushed back from her high white forehead, her face was calm but there was something terribly poignant in her dark eyes, gazing unseeingly at the ceiling. At last she looked down and our eyes met.

"In Venezuela," she said coolly, "they hung up four men

54

in front of Dr. O'Brien's house and cut pieces off them twice a day. That's his story, and he's stuck to it, winter and summer, for twelve years that *I* know of. You might as well get used to it. Oh God, what a mess!"

She got up and began to walk up and down in front of the fireplace. Then she sat down.

"That's funny too," she said.

I looked blankly at her. I hadn't noticed either what was funny then or anything funny before.

"I learned that from him," she said. "He always paced up and down when things got pretty foul. He was an awful old pirate, but I . . . I liked him. He was decent to me; and I'm telling you—for *your* information, I don't give a damn about the rest of them—that I wasn't his mistress. He never had one, or I guess I would have been."

I rather wished Dr. O'Brien would come back and tell me about Venezuela, but he wasn't anywhere in sight.

Agnes Hutton had returned to her study of the ceiling. I said, "It's too bad."

"You're telling me?"

"No, I'm not telling you. I'm just saying it's too bad he's dead, that's all."

But like Cheryl, I found I was thinking about Michael Spur, not about Mr. Trent. I glanced covertly at Agnes Hutton, wondering what she was really thinking about, looking up at the ceiling like that. Her hands were thrust deep into the pockets of her dressing gown, one knee was crossed on the other. She was quiet, rather, I thought, as a cat is quiet before it does something drastic about a bird. Now and then her free foot moved, the way a cat's tail moves and is still again.

"I suppose you'll want to get off to New York first thing in the morning," she said after a long time.

"I suppose so," I said. As a matter of fact I hadn't even thought of myself and what I was going to do. It seemed rather odd that she should have been thinking of it, when she must have had much more important things on her mind. For some reason, it made me a little uneasy. But I hadn't time until later to give it much thought, for just then somebody opened the library door and we heard Mr. Doyle's brisk business-like voice assuring Major Ellicott that everything would be taken care of with as little trouble as possible.

They came into the living room where Agnes and I were. Dr. Sartoris was with them, and I gathered from what was said that Mr. Doyle and Dr. O'Brien both agreed with him that Michael Spur should be left in his care until Mr. Doyle had talked the situation over with Judge Rose in the morning. Dr. O'Brien had certified the cause of death to have been a bullet that pierced the heart and caused instant death. He told Dr. Sartoris that he thought any doctor familiar with the case history would have predicted the present tragedy, and seemed in some way to imply that Mr. Trent had got about what was coming to him for not having taken the precautions that were suggested.

I don't think Mr. Archer liked it very much, seeing Dr. O'Brien so obviously impressed by the New York specialist, but he didn't say anything. His face got a couple of shades redder and he snorted twice. But no one paid any attention to him. Major Ellicott said that he hadn't realized the gravity of the situation, but that he was now willing to advise Mrs. Trent to go the limit in protecting Michael from the consequences of his folly. Agnes Hutton smiled her Mona Lisa smile at that. I didn't realize how funny it was. I found out shortly that the surest way to stop Mrs. Trent from doing anything was to have Major Ellicott suggest it to her. At the time his statement seemed very impressive to me. I thought Agnes was smiling just because she was rather horrid.

Mr. Archer and Dr. Sartoris went with Mr. Doyle to see Mrs. Trent. When they came down Dr. O'Brien, who had been talking quietly in the hall with Major Ellicott, went up again with Dr. Sartoris to give Cheryl a sedative. They must have given Michael something pretty stiff, because I heard Dr. O'Brien say he guessed that would hold him till morning, and Dr. Sartoris agreed that it certainly ought to.

It wasn't until they had their hats on and were leaving that Agnes Hutton brought up a point that was certainly sensible enough, but was rather startling at first, by asking Mr. Doyle if he wasn't going to lock the library.

Mr. Doyle looked surprised, and she explained that Mr. Trent kept a number of valuable papers there, and that he had always made a practice of locking the room at night, which, as it turned out, was perfectly untrue. However, Mr. Doyle locked it, and gave the key to Mr. Archer, who put it in a drawer in the hall table as soon as Dr. O'Brien's Ford coupé had rattled out of the drive.

Agnes watched Mr. Archer with her slow smile.

"That wasn't very clever of me after all, was it," she remarked, and shrugged her shoulders.

"I guess I'll go to bed. Coming?"

But I don't think she did go to bed. I heard her moving about in her room, next to mine, for a long time after I'd turned out my light, and when I woke up about five o'clock I heard her bath water running.

I lay there in Queen Elizabeth's bed, trying to think what she reminded me of. All I could think of was a white gardenia I once saw on the desk of the Police Commissioner in New York. It had enough high explosive tucked carefully in between its waxen petals to blow Ivy Hill into a million pieces.

EIGHT

It was eight o'clock when I woke again. The sun was streaming in, a cardinal was singing just outside, and Aspasia was standing there with my breakfast tray, with a single yellow tulip in a delicate silver vase next to a beautiful silver coffee pot, saying, "Good morning, miss. Where would you like your tray?"

It took me a long second to remember that Mr. Trent was downstairs, dead—murdered—and that Michael Spur and Cheryl Trent were waking from drugged forgetfulness to the tragic memory of the night before.

"I could put it on the table by the window, miss," Aspasia said and while she was doing it I got into my dressing gown and picked up the folded paper.

"It's not in the papers, miss," she said. "But Magothy found a reporter from Baltimore sittin' on the steps when I got up this mornin', so I reckon it'll be in today."

I nodded. Aspasia was a high yaller, and I suppose that accounted for her detached interest in her employer's murder.

"Of course," she added, pouring my coffee, "we wasn't surprised. Magothy locked all our doors last night, and he wouldn't go out this mornin', not until the Major knocked on the door his self. Is there anything else, miss?"

"Nothing, thanks," I said.

I was finishing my third cup of coffee when there was a tap on my door. I said "Come in," and was rather surprised when I saw Dr. Sartoris, in cool white linen, looking grave and formal.

"Forgive my disturbing you," he said, closing the door again and coming across the room. "May I sit down?"

"Why, yes . . . if you like," I said.

He sat down and lighted a cigarette.

"I've come from Mrs. Trent, Miss Cather," he said, looking at me; and I had exactly the same warm confused feeling about him that I'd had when he first spoke to me on the train. Except that I hadn't any make-up on my face to protect me from letting him see that he affected me just as he did Mrs. Trent, and Cheryl, and Agnes Hutton. He smiled ever so faintly, and I got perfectly furious—at myself for being stupid, and at him for . . . well, for knowing it. It seemed to me a shoddy sort of business, this going around and making women's hearts turn over, and all the rest of it, just for practice. It was like an animal trainer who couldn't ever go out without taking his giraffe along with him. Granting that making women fall in love with him, or at least fall heavily for him, is a psychoanalyst's stock in trade, or a psychotherapist's, as he called himself, it did annoy me very much that he couldn't drop it for five minutes. Or anyway, it annoyed me to find myself as susceptible to him as a sixteen-year-old.

"Do you enjoy having every woman you meet fall in love with you, Dr. Sartoris?" I asked, thinking I might just as well let him know that I wasn't being taken in, even if I couldn't prevent my heart from doing odd things when he looked at me.

He smiled.

"No," he said coolly. "As a matter of fact I don't. Frequently it's very annoying."

It seemed to me that he should at least have had grace enough to demur a little. But he didn't. In fact he said, "Are you planning to write the story of my great success?"

"I hadn't thought of it. Why?"

"Well, since you've put your finger on the only reason for it, I thought you might be analyzing me as possible material. Now that . . ."

He hesitated, and blew a suave blue funnel of smoke toward the window.

"Now that Mr. Trent is dead," I said. But his eyes were grave again.

"Mrs. Trent asked me to give you her sincere regards," he said almost abruptly; "and to tell you she knows you'll want to get away. There's a train at ten from the station down the road. She's ordered the car for you at nine-forty-five and is very sorry that your visit was interrupted so tragically. She hopes that she'll have the pleasure of seeing you some time in the future."

"Thank you, Dr. Sartoris," I said. "Will you give Mrs.

Trent my sincere regards, and tell her I'll be ready at a quarter of ten. Good-bye."

I held out my hand. He rose, and took it. Even then he couldn't forego pressing it just enough not to commit himself but to imply some way that there was a special bond between us. However, I'd got over my momentary lapse, and I saw him again as a handsome and charming charlatan —who, furthermore, was glad I was leaving.

"Good-bye, Miss Cather," he said very gently. "I enjoyed our train trip, yesterday."

"Good-bye," I said.

I poured the last few drops of coffee in the pot into my cup and drank it. I wanted to go back to New York. I hadn't the slightest desire to sleep another night in Queen Elizabeth's bed, or to watch Mrs. Trent making a fool of herself. But somehow I didn't like just being put out. Then I remembered my promise to Cheryl Trent, that I wouldn't go right away. But that was plainly out, in view of what had happened.

In the middle of my bath I suddenly thought of what Agnes Hutton had said about my going in the morning, and then I remembered what it was that had vaguely bothered me when she had said it. It was what I'd heard outside, when she had said to someone—some man—"If she's half as smart as she thinks she is," and the rest of it.

It would be interesting to know whom she was talking to, I thought. Then it occurred to me that it wouldn't do me any good if I did. I couldn't stay around when Mrs. Trent had ordered the car to remove me at 9.45.

I dressed and packed. At 9.30 I was about to put on my hat and go out to find Cheryl, when there was another rap at my door. This time it was Mr. Archer.

"Good morning," I said.

"Good morning, Miss Cather."

He was pink and well-shaved and glowing as usual, but the twinkle in his eyes was gone and he was very serious and business-like.

"I've arranged with Mr. Doyle, the State's Attorney, for you to be allowed to leave this morning," he said. "And I feel you deserve some little remuneration for your trip down. So I've taken the liberty of discharging that obligation of my friend's."

He handed me a piece of paper that I didn't quite realize was a check until I had it in my hands and saw the "Five

Hundred Dollars" written on it, and my name, and Mr. Archer's.

"Oh," I said, and handed it back to him. "I'm sorry—I didn't understand. I couldn't possibly take this. It's very kind of you, but I'm paid by my magazine."

He brushed my objections aside peremptorily.

"Nonsense," he said. "Put it in your purse. You deserve something. Call it damages, if you like. All you've been through down here. The car'll be around in ten minutes. You need any help? I'll send the maid up."

He started out.

"Just a minute, please, Mr. Archer," I said—rather sharply, I'm afraid, because he turned around and looked at me as if he were a little taken aback. "I'm afraid you don't understand. In the first place, I'm leaving for New York in fifteen minutes anyway. In the second, I don't accept gifts. Will you take this, or shall I tear it up?"

He took it and mumbled something about my being absurd, and went out.

It was almost time for Mrs. Trent's car to show up. I put on my hat and went downstairs to see if I could find Cheryl. Instead I found a telegram on the table in the hall. It was from one of the tabloids, offering me an even larger sum than Mr. Archer's check to cover the murder from the inside as a human interest story for the strap-hangers of the great city.

I had torn the yellow envelope open at one end. As I put the telegram back into it, I noticed that the flap was a little wavy, as thin paper is that's been wet and dried out again. Or steamed, I thought. I wondered who it was that was enough interested in my correspondence to go to all that trouble. It might have been Mrs. Trent—it couldn't have been Mr. Archer, because he would have met the offer it contained. That didn't leave a great many people, and as Michael Spur, to the best of my knowledge, had not left his room, it let him out as well as Mr. Archer. I wondered a bit about it, decided there was nothing to do anyway, and thought I might perhaps tell Cheryl about it, if I could find her.

All that went through my head in much less time than it takes to write it. And just when I had made up my mind that nothing could be done and it didn't matter anyway, I became suddenly aware of a curious smell of something burning. It seemed to come out of the living room, so I went across the hall and looked in. I was right, only it was a cigar that was burning, and the man smoking it seemed quite pleased with it, or with himself, or with something. He was standing in front of the Florentine fireplace. A very light gray hat was tilted on the extreme back of a shiny crop of wavy white hair, carefully parted in the middle. He had the cigar perched at a jaunty angle in the right corner of his mouth, and his mouth was set in a red, rugged and uneven face. His hands were thrust down into the pockets of his brown striped trousers; and he was jingling his cash, teetering methodically up and down on the balls of his feet, and surveying Mrs. Trent's living room with the air of a man who had just bought the whole works for about ten dollars cash.

"Oh," I said. "Pardon me. I thought I smelled something burning."

He chuckled.

"Lieutenant Kelly's the name," he said.

"I'm Louise Cather."

"Oh? You're the writer lady I heard about?"

"I nodded.

"You don't say?"

I nodded again.

"Well, well," said Lieutenant Kelly. He shook his head and made a clucking noise with his tongue as if it was all too much for him. Then he said suddenly, "What you got your hat on for?"

"I'm leaving," I said.

"Yeh? Where you going?"

"New York."

"Says who?"

I hesitated. I didn't quite like to say, "Says Dr. Sartoris and Mr. Archer," so I said, "Well, there's no point in my staying."

Lieutenant Kelly shook his head.

"Won't do, lady," he said. "Take off your hat and stick around till we see whether there's any point. You're the second person's tried to duck out on me."

"Really?"

"Yeh. The doctor fella—Sartoris—showed me a telegram from a society. I guess he said it's an ethical society. That sound all right? They have 'em in New York?"

"Yes. I guess they do."

"Well, they wanted him to lecture to 'em. I said he'd better get 'em to change the date. Say, there's a telegram for you out there—you get it?"

"Yes. I got it."

"Well, then. Just take off your things and make yourself comfortable."

"Listen, lieutenant," I said. "Mrs. Trent has ordered the car for me, and Mr. Doyle said it was all right for me to go. I don't quite see how I can stay."

He looked at me suspiciously.

"What's the hurry?" he demanded.

I told him Mrs. Trent had practically ordered me out, that it wasn't my idea.

He seemed interested, and nodded as if it seemed to have some meaning.

"Now look here, lady," he said. "I'm taking charge here, from now on, and what I say goes. You're taking orders from *me*, and nobody else. Now you go away somewheres, and I'll fix it up. O.K.?"

"O.K.," I said.

"All right, then. Now you might just tell me what you know about all this business."

"I'd like to ask you a question first."

"Shoot."

"You're a detective, aren't you?"

"That's right. Lieutenant Joseph J. Kelly, Bureau of Detectives, Baltimore Police Department."

"But that isn't my question. I want to know what you're here for?"

He grinned.

"I ain't sure I can tell you that."

"Do you think Michael Spur didn't shoot Mr. Trent?"

"Why, lady," he said very blandly, "I ain't even said he *did* shoot him, have I?"

"No. But everybody just assumes naturally he did. I'm sure he thinks so too."

"Well, I guess he ought to know."

"Oh, no!" I said quickly. "That's just the point."

"Now look here," he said. "Let's get this straight, so we don't have no trouble understanding each other. I ain't taking anybody's say-so about anything, till I see what's up. Got it?"

"Yes."

"All right, then. We're set."

He sat down, and I sat down too.

"Now, then. How long you been here?"

"I came yesterday evening, about seven."

"Yeh? What for, now?"

"I thought you knew."

He grinned.

"No. I don't know nothing."

So I told him why I was there. When I finished he said, "You didn't know any of 'em before you came down?"

"Not a one," I said.

He nodded.

"Now," he said, "they say you found the body."

It was surprising how quickly Mr. Trent's colorful, sharp, determined personality had evaporated, and left just "the body" in its place.

I told him how I couldn't sleep, and had come down to get the magazine I'd seen that evening on the sofa where we were sitting, and had heard someone talking in the library. He nodded, and chewed his under lip when I told him about seeing Michael Spur out on the terrace.

"He see you?" he asked.

"No, I'm sure he didn't, because he didn't turn around, and I got out and back upstairs as quick as I could."

Then I told him how I'd rigged myself up a card table and was playing solitaire because I couldn't go to sleep.

He nodded at that too. "Country's a noisy damn place when those frogs get going," he said.

"It was just two when I heard a shot," I went on. "I got up and came down and found Mr. Trent. He was dead. I'd just started to look around when the light went off."

"What's that?" he said quickly. He acted as if he hadn't quite heard me.

"The lights went off."

"While you was standing there?"

He got up.

"That's enough," he said. "You're *staying*."

He thought a minute. Then he reached in his coat pocket and took out a folded newspaper, which he handed to me. I opened it. On the front page there was a three-column picture of a girl on a horse, erect, smiling, perfectly poised, taking a hedge. It was headed "Daughter of Slain Millionaire at Valley Horse Show." Under it was a brief account of the mere fact that Duncan Trent, millionaire shipbuilder and capitalist, had been found dead in the library of his country home on the Chesapeake near Annapolis, and that Mr. Thomas Doyle, the State's Attorney, was in charge of investigations. It went on with a short summary of Mr. Trent's life and his sudden rise to wealth during and after the War. There was also an article headed "Fatal Shooting Recalled." It told how Mr. Trent's partner Stephen Spur was shot and killed by his son Michael fourteen years before, and added that Michael Spur was present at the Trents' estate, Ivy Hill, last night.

I handed the paper back to Lieutenant Kelly.

"I feel kinda sorry for that girl," he said. I nodded.

"I got all the local reporters on the outside looking in," he added. He was looking at the picture.

"Kinda pretty, ain't she? I got a girl of my own about her age."

He stopped abruptly and looked towards the door. I turned. It was Cheryl, but she didn't look like the millionaire's daughter on the horse. She was erect and poised, but the look of assured confidence was gone. Her yellow hair looked almost white above her face that was like old ivory now that the warmth was drained out of it. Her eyes were like two blue splotches of cobalt sky mirrored in a pool. I supposed the bright slash of defiant crimson of her lips was to keep up her courage, or perhaps it was just habit, like putting on stockings.

"Hello!" she said. "Perry said you'd gone—I'm so glad you haven't."

"No, I'm staying a while, it seems," I said. "This is Lieutenant Kelly, from Baltimore. This is Miss Trent, Lieutenant."

"Pleased to meet you, Miss Trent," he said, and put out a large red hand. "I sure am mighty sorry about all this."

There was something awfully decent the way he said it as if he really meant it. Cheryl took his hand and shook it without saying a word.

"I suddenly wanted to cry," she told me in her room a little later. "He was so sort of . . . sort of sweet—you know?"

"Thanks," she said, after a while. "Major Ellicott said you were down here, and my mother sent me down to tell you she wants the . . . the case left in Mr. Doyle's hands, or Dr. Sartoris's. He's a specialist in mental cases."

"I see," said Lieutenant Kelly.

"You see, Mother feels that Mr. Doyle understands Michael's difficulty, and she doesn't want anything dreadful to happen to him."

"I see," said Lieutenant Kelly again. "So that's the way of it, is it? Well, Miss Trent, I wouldn't worry about it if I was you. You just run up and tell your mother Mr. Doyle's going to be out pretty soon and we'll fix it all up."

Cheryl looked up at him, her blue eyes swimming in tears.

"Oh, really? Then you won't send him to Phipps?"

Lieutenant Kelly looked puzzled.

"Phipps? Oh. No, I don't guess we'll send him to Phipps."

"I'll tell Mother," she said quickly. "She'll be so glad."

Lieutenant Kelly looked after her. He screwed his face sideways, scratched his head with his free hand, and looked at me.

"What's Phipps?" I asked.

"That's the nut clinic at Johns Hopkins," he said simply. "But that ain't exactly what I meant," he added.

"What did you mean?"

"Well—I guess I might as well tell you, and you can break it easy to the little girl. If we send Spur anywhere it ain't going to be Phipps. It's going to be jail."

"Jail!" I said.

"Yeh. Jail."

"What for, for heaven's sake?"

"For murder, lady," he said. "Now listen. I don't say there ain't a lot in this psychopathy—I'm as up to date as any of 'em—but it don't sound reasonable to me for a bird that's been all right for fourteen years to come along and shoot the only person in the house that ought to be shot."

I stared at him.

"Ought to be shot?" I repeated.

"I mean . . . Well, we'll just let things work out their own way. O.K.?"

I nodded.

"All right," he said. "If I was you I'd go up and have a chat with Miss Trent. We're going to be mighty busy down here for a while."

A lot of men with cameras and things had come and were in the hall. When I went upstairs Lieutenant Kelly was shaking hands with Mr. Doyle, who had also just arrived.

NINE

I went upstairs, but I didn't go to see Cheryl—not then. I went into my own room and changed from a suit into a dress. Then I wrote a letter to Mr. McCrae. After that I stood at my window watching Perry Bassett. He was on his knees, weeding the enormous crescent-shaped bed of yellow and red and mauve and pink and white and mottled tulips just below my window. He was dressed in an old mud-stained pair of riding breeches and a tweed coat out at one elbow, and he had on an old brown bowler, and looked about as much as if he was in mourning for his murdered brother-in-law as Dr. Sartoris did in his jaunty white linens.

I was watching him move foot by foot along the edge of the tulip bed, thinking among other things that he certainly didn't look like a man who had cast two fortunes into the Grand Canyon at the foot of Manhattan, when Aspasia came in.

"Major Ellicott wants to know if he can speak to you, Miss?"

Since I had already interviewed Mrs. Trent's doctor and Mr. Trent's lawyer, in various stages of undress, there was no reason for getting choicey (as Aspasia said later about something quite different).

I was a little surprised at his looks when he came in. I'd forgot that he was really a very attractive person, not particularly old—in fact, he looked much younger in a dark blue lounge suit than he had in dinner clothes. And he didn't bother about closing the door, as my other callers had.

"Good morning, Miss Cather," he said. "I hope you got a little rest last night, though I can hardly believe it. In fact I was going to suggest last night that if you moved a pillow onto the floor you'd find it more comfortable."

I laughed.

"I'm quite a Spartan."

"I believe it," he returned seriously. "However, there's no reason for your being involved any further in our troubles. I've talked it over with Mr. Doyle—knowing you'd want to get away. He agrees with me that there's no earthly sense in your staying here any longer. I've arranged for a car to run you up to Baltimore in time for you to get the noon train to New York."

Then he noticed my strapped bags.

"Oh. You're packed?"

"Yes, I'm all packed, but Lieutenant Kelly said I was to stay."

He smiled.

"Like a policeman," he said. "Don't let that worry you. Doyle said you were to go. I'll have your things put in the car."

"Thanks very much," I said, and suppressed an insane desire to laugh boisterously.

He turned to go. Apparently, I thought, he wasn't going to *pay* me to get me out of the way. For a moment my stock seemed pretty low. But I was wrong. He turned as if it were a second thought, and one that he didn't quite like to discuss with a lady.

"As soon as Mrs. Trent recovers a little from the shock of last night's tragedy, Miss Cather," he said, "we hope you'll accept a . . . a token of our appreciation for your kindness and understanding."

He smiled ironically.

"I won't say for the beastly lot of annoyance you've been put to."

"That's very nice of you," I said.

After he'd closed the door I tried to figure out what all this was about, and what I really should do. If Mr. Doyle and the family were ordering me out, Lieutenant Kelly and my own increasing curiosity as to what it was all about didn't seem enough, really, to keep me here. So far Agnes Hutton, Mrs. Trent, Dr. Sartoris, Mr. Archer and Major Ellicott had suggested my going. I thought it seemed a majority vote.

There was a discreet tap on my door, and I glanced around and said "Come." Perry Bassett slipped in, and stood turning his musty brown bowler around in his hands, making a little shower of dried soil on the floor. He looked exactly like a frightened rabbit.

This time I did laugh. I couldn't help it.

"Don't tell me you've arranged to have a car for me in fifteen minutes, Mr. Bassett," I said; and he looked very blank and said, "Oh, dear!"

"I've got three offers of transportation already," I went on. "Unless you're prepared with something pretty good I don't think you can meet them."

"I . . . I really don't know what you mean," he said nervously. "I just . . . just came to tell you my sister has asked me to say she's very sorry about . . . everything, and she hopes very much you can stay on with us. On account of my niece, Miss Cather. She's very lonesome, and I'm afraid she's going to be very unhappy."

"Oh," I said. I looked at him intently, wondering if he was telling the truth about Mrs. Trent. If he was it made a lot of difference. That would mean that Dr. Sartoris had deliberately lied to get me away. But I didn't believe it. Not that I put it past Dr. Sartoris. But he wouldn't have done it that way if it had been his idea. He'd have done it the way Major Ellicott did, arranged to have me taken to Baltimore to the train, not dumped out at a trolley station by the road. However, there was something very honest and appealing in the rabbity little man in front of me.

"Did you know that your sister ordered a car for me this morning, to take me away at quarter of ten?" I asked gently.

He looked nervously down at his hands and put them behind him, and said "Oh, dear!" again. Then he looked at me and smiled like a child caught in a perfectly well-meant lie.

"You see, Miss Cather," he said timidly, "my sister sometimes forgets what she ought to do, but she doesn't really mean any harm by it. I'll just speak to her. I think she really wants you to stay. You will, won't you?"

"Yes, Mr. Bassett," I said. "I think I will."

I had a strong suspicion, from my few minutes' talk with Lieutenant Kelly, that in spite of Mr. Doyle I didn't have much chance of getting away. It seemed to me that other people around were rather underestimating Lieutenant Kelly—and that turned out to be very much truer than I thought at the time.

When Perry Bassett went out into the hall I caught a glimpse of Lieutenant Kelly and Mr. Doyle going into Michael Spur's room. As they closed the door Perry Bassett said "Tch tch," and shook his head. He went on downstairs.

I was still standing there, thinking about all of it, when Dr. Sartoris came from the other end of the hall. I thought he looked rather surprised to see me still about, but he merely nodded and went into Michael's room.

A few minutes later Aspasia came and told me Mrs. Trent would like to see me.

"Her room's this way, miss," she said, and I followed her toward the end of the hall from which Dr. Sartoris had come, and into a wide transverse hall corresponding to the one in the other wing except that there was no balcony here. There was, however, a knight in armor on the landing of the wide staircase. He looked very cocky and had on a plumed helmet. The plume was quite new.

A number of doors opened off the hall. I gathered that this wing contained the family apartments. Aspasia opened the last door at the end of the corridor nearest the bay, and I found myself looking into a large sunny room with pale coral walls and apple green woodwork and a deep mauve velvet carpet.

Mrs. Trent, excited and obviously upset, was pacing the floor in the empty space in front of the door. Cheryl was sitting, her chin on her hand, gazing unhappily out the window.

"Come in, Miss Mather."

Cheryl looked slowly up at her mother, then shrugged her shoulders as if she knew it was hopeless, and turned away.

"I want you to tell me what they're going to do," Mrs. Trent demanded abruptly, and went on without waiting for me to answer. "I don't understand Mr. Doyle. What is the matter with him? I've explained to him, and I've had Victor —Dr. Sartoris—explain to him. It seems to me he's just making this as hard for me as he can. Why is he acting like this?"

"I'm afraid he can't help it, Mrs. Trent," I said, sitting down in an elaborate yellow satin Empire chair with swans' necks for arms. I glanced around the room. If you'd known it was going to be French you could have guessed all of it before you went in, the profusion of trivial knick-knacks and the piles of lace and satin cushions and spindly-legged dolls in the yellow satin chaise longue in front of the fireplace. On the low table by it was an enormous pink satin box of chocolates, open, with empty little brown paper cups scattered untidily about. A movie magazine was turned face down beside it. It struck me as being utterly heartless, in some way, but very like Mrs. Trent. She acted as if her

70

husband's death was some sort of a tiresome interlude, the only purpose of which was to annoy her.

"He could certainly help it if he wanted to," she snapped pettishly. "I'll give him some money. He'll do something about it."

"Oh, mother!" said Cheryl in a low voice. Even knowing Mrs. Trent I was aghast.

"Well, I will. He's a politician, isn't he?"

She stopped her pacing and held out her hands in a gesture of impotence.

"But I can't *get* any money!" she said. "That's the whole trouble. Archer won't give me any. I've asked him."

"You don't need any money, mother," Cheryl said patiently.

Her mother picked up a paper from her desk and held it up. It was an announcement of the public auction of a property by court order to recover a mortgage, scheduled for Saturday at eleven o'clock at the courthouse steps in Annapolis.

"I'm going to buy this," Mrs. Trent said. "That's what I need money for. And I'm going to have it."

Cheryl looked at the printed bill.

"It's the Foster property up the river," Mrs. Trent went on. "It's just what Victor needs for his sanatorium. Fifty acres, a dairy, water front, twenty rooms. They're selling it day after tomorrow, and I'm going to buy it for him."

"Mother!" Cheryl said gently. "Didn't Dad say you shouldn't buy it—that we couldn't afford it now?"

Mrs. Trent's mouth closed tightly. She said nothing, but her manner said plainly, "Your father is dead. It's none of his business."

Cheryl bit her lip and turned toward the window.

Mrs. Trent turned suddenly to me.

"You'll bid it in for me, Miss Mather. That's an idea. Go as high as you have to. It's what Victor needs. And it's so close —only a few miles away."

The thought came to me suddenly that I was staring in astonishment at an insane woman.

"I'll get the money, you needn't worry about that," she said firmly.

She pressed a bell in the wall and began moving about restlessly, absorbed in her new idea, until a colored maid came.

"Tell Mr. Archer I want to see him at once, Lucy," she ordered, and began her pacing again, utterly oblivious of me sitting there or of her daughter, wan and unhappy, staring out the window.

Mr. Archer came. I was surprised at that; I thought he wouldn't. And he looked at me in surprise; apparently he also thought I'd gone. He stood just inside the door, without saying a word, until his eyes fell on the bill of sale of the Foster property up the river. Then he gave a disgusted snort and glared at Mrs. Trent.

"As long as I'm in charge of Duncan's estate, Emily," he said, "you're not going to throw his money away on this sort of thing."

He tapped the bill sharply with a pudgy forefinger.

"It's my money!" Mrs. Trent retorted defiantly. "You can't keep it away from me!"

Mr. Archer glared at her a moment, then, like Cheryl, gave up.

"I haven't looked at Duncan's will recently, Emily," he said quietly.

"He couldn't cut me out of his will! I have a dower right, and that's one-third of the estate at the very least!"

Mr. Archer laughed a little.

"That's true, Emily. But I don't know how much one-third of the estate is going to be. Duncan lost a great deal of money in nineteen-twenty-nine."

Mrs. Trent's jaw dropped. She stared at him, breathing heavily.

"What do you mean?" she said at last.

"I mean that the estate has shrunk," he said sharply. "Duncan's death will make it shrink more. I don't know that you can afford to keep Sartoris any longer. That's what I mean."

He got up and went to the door, and turned with his hand on the knob. He looked steadily at Mrs. Trent with barely concealed contempt, his face purple with suppressed anger.

"Doyle's coming back after lunch," he said curtly. "He'll want to talk to you."

She gaped stupidly.

"To me?"

"To you. Someone murdered your husband, Emily."

Even Mrs. Trent winced at the devastating contempt in his voice.

"It was Michael Spur!" she cried. "It wasn't . . . murder!"

"Do you *know* it was Michael Spur?" he said coldly.

She stared speechless at him. Then she faltered, "Why, yes, Tom! Everybody does! Dr. Sartoris . . . *you* know it!"

"I *don't* know it, Emily," Mr. Archer said dryly. "What's more, the police don't seem to."

He opened the door and slammed it behind him. The long crystals on the candlesticks on the mantel tinkled nervously under the impact.

TEN

The three of us stared blankly at the white solid surface of the door. Mrs. Trent, oddly enough, recovered first. "Well!" she said. "Whatever do you suppose he means by that?"

Cheryl had leaned forward tensely.

"Louise!" she gasped, light dawning in her wide-open hyacinth eyes. "Does he mean that maybe Michael didn't . . . do it? Didn't kill my father?"

"Nonsense!" Mrs. Trent snapped. "Of course he did it. If he didn't do it, it means somebody else did; and that means . . . murder."

She hesitated, and then repeated the word sharply, very much as if she were shocked but determined not to be afraid.

"Murder."

She looked at me.

"Nobody would murder my husband," she said, her voice high and edged with a kind of fear and suspense, rather as if she wanted me to deny it if I dared. "Would they—you."

It was obvious that she was speaking to me, and I don't know but that I'd quite as soon be called "you" as Miss Mather. So I said, "No one that I know of, Mrs. Trent."

"You see, Cheryl. She says Michael did it."

"No, she didn't, mother!" Cheryl said quickly.

I was astonished at the change in her. When I came in she was like a drooping water lily lying on a bank in the sun. Now her golden head was high, her lips parted breathlessly, her eyes bright. I don't mean that she was happy. She wasn't; but she was alive again and eager.

"Yes, she did!"

Mrs. Trent turned back to me pettishly.

"My brother says you've been talking to that policeman from Baltimore."

"Yes."

"What did he say, Louise?" Cheryl demanded quickly.

There was no use in trying to evade the point, and anyway Lieutenant Kelly had told me to break the news. This seemed as good a time as any, with Mr. Archer having prepared the way.

"I may as well tell you, Mrs. Trent," I sad, "that Lieutenant Kelly feels there *is* a possibility that Mr. Trent's death wasn't accidental. That he actually *was* murdered."

"You mean that Michael . . . that he wasn't just walking around in his unconscious libido when he did it?"

"That's evidently it," I said.

I glanced at Cheryl. She was standing up, slim and straight; her face was pale, but the brave light was still in her eyes. She was moving her head slowly back and forth. I could almost hear her murmuring "I don't believe it, I don't believe it."

"Well, in that case," said Mrs. Trent, shrugging her shoulders and reaching for the box of chocolates, "they'd better take him out of here at once. The sooner he gets away the sooner we'll have a little peace."

Cheryl moved quickly across the room.

"Mother!" she cried passionately, stamping her foot on the floor. "How can you bear to talk like that? I won't listen to it! You've no right to say such things!"

A deep strangled sob choked her last words as she burst out of the room.

Mrs. Trent looked at me with genuine dumfounded amazement on her flabby carefully made-up face.

"Well, I declare," she said. "What's got into her?"

She sat down and picked up her magazine.

"You'd better go see," she went on helplessly. "I've given up trying to understand that child."

I started toward the door.

"Wait a minute," she said. "My brother says he thinks you ought to stay here a while. So it'll be all right."

"Thanks very much," I said, with what I regarded as devastating sarcasm.

"That's all right," she said vapidly, turning a page. I heard her hand fishing absently among the crisp brown paper cups in her box of chocolates as I closed the door.

"What a woman!" I thought.

I found Cheryl's room by the simple process of opening every door until I came to it. It was at the other end of the corridor. A narrow passage ran between it and the railing around the stair well. It was a charming room, finished in ivory and blue, and a good decorator had managed to use Pompadour chintz at the mullioned windows without being ridiculous. Cheryl was standing at one of them, looking down into the gardens. She was quite calm, and when I came in she said, "I'm sorry I made a scene, Louise. But Mother can be so provoking."

It seemed to me to be putting it mildly.

"You *are* going to stay, aren't you?" she said, coming over and sitting down in one end of a deep chintz-covered sofa. She tossed me a pillow and a cigarette and I sat down at the other end.

"Perry came and gave Mother the devil. He's the only one on earth who can manage her, you know. And she said she'd ask you to stay. I don't want you to go. I . . . I don't feel quite so alone . . ."

"Well," I said briskly, "I'm staying. I have to, in the first place. Lieutenant Kelly said so. He's not letting anybody leave right now. Afterwards we'll see."

"Listen," she said. "What Mr. Archer said. What do you think about it?"

"I don't know, Cheryl," I returned. "I don't think I'd count on *anything*, if I were you."

She laughed unhappily.

"Don't worry. I know that. But *I don't believe he did it.* I just don't, some way. I mean I don't think he'd *do* it."

"Do you think anybody else would?"

Something behind her eyes made them flatten curiously, and took all the velvety quality away, and left them cold and vindictive.

"I'd better not say—had I?"

Her voice was so hard and so mature that I had to think to make myself remember that she was only twenty. Then I remembered that Constance Kent had murdered her brother when she was sixteen, and that Lady Jane Grey had been named Queen of England, convicted of high treason and beheaded all during her seventeenth year. Age doesn't make much difference in the way a woman acts. It's the propelling force that counts.

"I mean somebody did do it," she said, still in that same hard little voice, "and I can think of several people who might have. Don't you see, it's got to be one of three things. Either it was Michael walking in his libido, as Mother calls it, just as Victor said he would. Or Michael did it in his right mind, for some reason he had that we don't know. Or third, somebody else did it."

76

I agreed with that.

"Well," she said more calmly, "it might be the first. I'm as sure as I'm sitting here that it isn't the second. I think it's the third, Louise. It's somebody that had a grudge against my father and knew Michael would get the blame for it."

She got up and walked across to her taffeta-skirted dressing table, leaned over and powdered her nose.

"In fact," she went on, "I'll bet anything I've got on Agnes Hutton."

I was a little startled, because exactly the same idea was passing through my own mind when she said it.

"Don't be absurd," I said. "Just because you don't like the woman is no reason to think she's a criminal."

She tossed her powder puff back into the enameled French make-up box and faced me, with admirable if slightly obstinate loyalty.

"I'll never believe Michael did it," she repeated simply. Then suddenly her defiance faded out, and she was a wistful, rather pathetic little figure trying hard to keep her courage up.

"Oh, Louise, please don't think I'm dreadful . . . but I'm *awfully* fond of Michael. Ever since I was a little girl I've adored him. They used to have that silly picture of Sir Galahad at school—you know the one with the horse and the armor? I used to pretend it was Michael. One day the other girls went to Boston to the theater, and I stayed behind with one other ratty mutt from the third form who'd done something too. I was supposed to do French verbs, but I sat there pretending Michael galloped in a fine suit of armor with a new pink plume in his helmet. I had an idea the picture was winking at me, and that Michael thought it was pretty stuffy too."

She laughed.

"I suppose that's what Dr. Sartoris calls 'escape,'" she said. "It sounds like frightful wash, but I guess it's what comes of growing up always bumping into Mother's iron men and never seeing any real ones. Anyway," she continued decisively, "I don't believe Michael murdered my father. He couldn't have—do you see?"

"I see perfectly," I said, and I did. I saw that Cheryl had an image of Michael in her heart that probably Sir Galahad himself couldn't have lived up to with all the new plumes in Christendom in his helmet.

I said, "You're going to marry Major Ellicott, aren't you?"

"Oh . . . yes. Of course. I'd almost forgotten that," she said. "In June."

"Well," I said, getting up, "June's a long way off. Why don't you go talk to Michael? It might cheer him up to find out you don't think he did it."

"Do you think he . . . wouldn't mind?"

I was surprised and I must have looked it, because she said, "You see, he always thought I was a terrible nuisance, always tagging along and getting in his way, scaring off the ducks or getting him stung with sea nettles or something. I wouldn't want to bother him."

"I don't think he'd mind," I said, without even smiling. Ridiculous as it seemed, Cheryl still thought of Michael as twenty and herself as six. I suppose that's why the idea of marrying Major Ellicott in June didn't seem to bother her at all. The two things were wholly unrelated. I wondered if Major Ellicott and Michael would be able to see it that way.

I left her at the door of Michael's sitting room and went to my own room. About ten minutes later Magothy knocked at my door and said that Lieutenant Kelly and Mr. Doyle wanted to see me in the dining room.

I went out and met Cheryl just closing Michael's door behind her. She was white and stunned.

"It's terrible, Louise!" she whispered. "He just sat there with his head in his hands, and he told me to go away. I didn't mind that, but the way he said it . . . as if he couldn't bear the sight of me."

Before I could say anything Magothy appeared at the other end of the hall.

"Miss Cherry," he said, "they done takin' pictures of yo' fingers in the dinin' room. Mistuh Doyle, he wants to know is yo' comin' down or is they comin' up?"

"I'll come down," she said.

"Yes, miss—thank yo', miss."

Major Ellicott met us at the foot of the stairs and took possession of Cheryl, rather sweetly, I thought. When she had placed first her right fingers and right thumb, then her left fingers and left thumb on the paper that one of Lieutenant Kelly's men prepared for her, he went out with her. I heard her say, "It's nice to be with you again, Dick. Where have you been?"

"Next, miss," said the man at the table—they called him "Skip" and it may have been his name. I stepped up and made my ten smudges that looked criminal on the face of them.

"That's the lot, sir," he said. "Except the old lady. I'll get her upstairs."

"O.K.," said Lieutenant Kelly, "Get going."

He turned to me.

"Know anything about shorthand?"

"A little. I'm not very fast."

"You can help us out, then," he said. "My man's had a blow-out on the road."

"All right," I said. "I'll do my best."

"O.K. Skip, tell Lynch to bring young Spur down. Get going."

ELEVEN

That's how I happened to hear as much of the testimony as I did. At that it's rather disquieting to realize how very little I knew of what was actually going on behind the hard-bitten red countenance of the gentleman from the Baltimore Bureau of Detectives. There was a certain vague feeling of satisfaction in the fact that Mr. Doyle didn't know it either.

Sergeant Lynch came down with Michael. I was a little shocked at the change in him. He looked like a man who had gone through the seven circles of hell. His face was drawn and gray beneath the almost mahogany layer of sun tan; his eyes were dark haunted hollows. He kept moistening his lips feverishly and throwing away one half-smoked cigarette after another.

"Sit down, Mr. Spur," said Lieutenant Kelly. He watched Michael intently, without moving his head. I recalled then who it was that Lieutenant Kelly reminded me of. It was an old chimpanzee in the London Zoo; he had very intelligent gray eyes that followed you around through a stubby fringe of colorless lashes, and looked as old and wise as sin, and about as sympathetic. Otherwise the resemblance was not very strong. The chimpanzee's hair was thin and rather ratty.

On the whole, however, I thought Lieutenant Kelly was very considerate. He said he wanted to get to the bottom of things, and wanted to know what Michael had been doing and how he'd happened to come back to Ivy Hill, and what he had done that night.

Michael said he had been with an engineering outfit building a dam in Arizona for the last six years. He'd got a degree in engineering from the University of California in 1925. The job was practically over, and he'd come to New York to see about tying up with a crowd of younger men who were doing some port construction in the Near East. That's when he had decided to drop down to Baltimore and run out to see the Trents.

Lieutenant Kelly asked him if the decision was very sudden, and he said no.

Lieutenant Kelly produced a telegram and handed it to him.

"You recognize this?"

"Yes. I sent it."

"Why'd you send it at two A.M.?"

Michael said he had been to a party, had taken a girl home, and happened to run across a telegraph office that was open, and sent it.

"Were you tight?" Lieutenant Kelly asked.

"Not very."

"But you didn't just make up your mind on the spur of the moment to come down?"

Michael hesitated. The door opened, and Mr. Archer came in. He was in a little better humor than the last time I'd seen him, but he had, it developed, strong ideas on the way Mr. Doyle was allowing things to be done.

"If Spur is—as I understand he is—practically accused of murder," he said, "this questioning is irregular to say the least."

There was some rather heated discussion between the two of them, during which Lieutenant Kelly looked calmly on through his white eyelashes. It was ended by Michael's saying positively that he understood he didn't have to make any statement but he wanted to get the thing cleared up; and Lieutenant Kelly went back to his last question, which I read from my notes.

Michael answered promptly that he had been thinking of coming ever since he'd left the West Coast, but hadn't made up his mind until that night.

"You did come entirely of your own free will."

I thought Michael hesitated again, but maybe I was wrong. He said, "Oh, entirely."

Lieutenant Kelly explained that what he was getting at was this: was there any outside reason for his coming—was he summoned by anyone, or what?

"No," said Michael. "Not a bit."

"You ever think of coming back before?"

"Often. But I was out West, and busy. I never got around to it before."

"Now then," said Lieutenant Kelly. "When you decided to come down here, did the idea of it make you nervous? I mean, figuring this Dr. Sartoris is right, did you have any idea that coming back would be hard on you?"

"Not if you mean did I think I'd have another attack of my old . . . illness, if you can call it that. I've not had any trouble for years. None that I've known of. I've always been careful not to keep a gun in my kit, but . . ."

"Eh?" said Lieutenant Kelly, looking up. "What's that?"

"I mean that since I shot my father, I've never had a gun in my possession."

"Did you know there was a gun in this house?"

Michael hesitated.

"Yes," he said.

"Whereabouts?"

"In the library, in the drawer of the table where Mr. Trent was sitting."

"How'd you know there was one there?"

Michael pressed out his cigarette in the ashtray, his fingers as taut as steel springs.

"I can't answer that," he said curtly.

"But you did know it was there?"

"Yes."

I saw Mr. Doyle and Mr. Archer exchange glances.

"Now, then," said Lieutenant Kelly. "When you got down here, how did everything strike you?"

Michael laughed shortly. He shrugged his shoulders, thrust his hands deep in his trousers pockets, sank his chin down on his chest and slouched down on his spine with his legs stretched out.

"It all seemed downright crazy," he said thickly. "Not a damn thing was changed except that Aunt Emily had got fat and Cheryl had got tall. Everything else was just the same. Perry, and Dick Ellicott. Mr. Trent and Mr. Archer here. Even Agnes Hutton. And old Magothy and all the tin suits stuck around. It gave me a queer feeling that I'd just dreamed everything. I felt if I'd look up suddenly I'd see Dad coming in the room."

Mr. Doyle nodded at Mr. Archer with complete finality, but Lieutenant Kelly seemed unimpressed.

"You tell anybody that, Mr. Spur?" he asked.

"Yes. I told Mr. Trent, and Miss Cather."

Lieutenant Kelly looked at me. I nodded.

"Anybody else?"

"Dr. Sartoris, when he looked in before I went to bed."

"All right," said Lieutenant Kelly. "Now, then. What time'd you get here?"

"I got off the trolley in Annapolis about eight-thirty and got a taxi. About nine, I guess."

"What time'd you go to bed?"

"I went upstairs about quarter to eleven and read a little. I don't know when I went to sleep, I was dead on my feet. Perry Bassett gave me a couple of pills to make me sleep."

"You usually take pills to make you sleep?"

He grinned suddenly.

"Not out West on an engineering job. You slave in the sun all day and you don't need 'em. I used to, when I was here."

"All right. Just tell us the rest of it."

Lieutenant Kelly crossed one carefully creased leg with a shiny yellow boot at the end of it.

"That's all there is," Michael said simply. "I'd had a night cap with Mr. Trent, about a quarter to eleven, said good night to him and went to my room. Dr. Sartoris came in and said we might have a talk in the morning. Perry Bassett came in and brought the pills. I went to bed, read a while, had another drink, and went to sleep. I slept—as far as I know—until I heard the row outside in the hall and found out Mr. Trent was dead."

"To the best of your knowledge you weren't out of your room after eleven o'clock?"

"I wasn't out of my room until I heard the noise in the hall."

"O.K.," said Lieutenant Kelly. "Now, lady, if you can type that out I'd like Mr. Spur to sign it. Just read it off, will you?"

I read it, rather haltingly.

Michael nodded. "That's right," he said.

"All right, then, Mr. Spur. I guess that'll be all. Have 'em get the doctor fellow."

We waited—I looking over my notes and writing bits in before I forgot them, Lieutenant Kelly paring his nails with the gold knife on one end of the heavy gold chain he wore festooned across his stomach, Mr. Doyle shuffling papers impatiently—until there was a rap on the door. I looked up expecting to see Dr. Sartoris. Instead it was Sergeant Lynch.

"The gun ain't showed up, chief," he said. "But I found something here."

He had a dark bundle in his hands, and he deposited it carefully on the end of the table.

I tried to look around Mr. Doyle's lank form to see what it was.

"Yeh?" said Lieutenant Kelly. I could tell by his voice that he was interested.

"It looks like blood, all right," said Mr. Doyle. "Hold it up, Kelly. Is there any more?"

"It's just over the right sleeve," said Sergeant Lynch.

I stood up so I could see too, and sat down again abruptly. It was my dressing gown they were looking at.

"Well, well," said Lieutenant Kelly. "Where'd you find it?"

"It was all folded up and packed in the bottom of a woman's suitcase. I guess she was making a getaway. Maid says it belongs to Miss Louise Cather—she's the New York woman."

Lieutenant Kelly and Mr. Doyle turned around and stared at me. Mr. Doyle seemed quite excited, and a rather ominous look came into his eyes, which were unpleasant enough anyway.

"So *that's* what's up, is it?" he said.

I hadn't noticed that Dr. Sartoris had come in until he spoke up now and said, "Don't be a damn fool, Doyle." It was the first impolite thing I had heard him say. It was neither suave nor imposing. I stared at him through a fog of bewilderment.

Mr. Doyle was very much annoyed, and Sergeant Lynch came to his defense.

"Damn fool, is he?" he said coolly. "Well, what's more, there's blood all over the window sill in her room. Let's see you laugh that off, big boy."

TWELVE

I looked helplessly at Lieutenant Kelly. He was examining the sleeve of my gown quite calmly and without any apparent excitement. I didn't know him well enough at that time to know that he never got excited, or that if he did there was never any evidence of it, or any change in his sober matter-of-fact habit of taking everything as it came and doing the best he could with it. I was so glad he was there that I could have cried, almost. It seemed to me that Mr. Doyle would be delighted to fix this affair on somebody outside the family circle. As a matter of fact, if I'd known what was in Lieutenant Kelly's mind I'd have seen that I was just as good a suspect as anybody, for his purposes. As it was, of course I felt I couldn't be seriously suspected.

He handed me the dressing gown.

"This yours?" he said.

"Yes."

"How long's that been on there?"

"I never saw it before in my life."

"How'd it get there?"

"I don't know. I didn't go near Mr. Trent, and I didn't touch anything when I ran across the library. Anyway, that sleeve was on the outside—I mean it was away from the body—because I ran between the table and the fireplace."

He grunted.

"We'll just go up and have a look," he said. "Excuse us a minute, doctor."

I glanced at Dr. Sartoris to let him know I was grateful to him for coming to my defense. But he was standing there in front of the fireplace, calmly blowing a long column of cigarette smoke ceilingward, as if the whole thing were an unconscionable bore. I didn't know then that his belongings had been searched as thoroughly as mine had. As I learned later, two men had come from Baltimore shortly after ten o'clock, and having begun in the library, were searching the entire house. So far the only thing that had turned up was my blood-stained silk dressing gown.

I went upstairs with the two policemen. Sergeant Lynch pointed with some personal satisfaction to the dark smear on my window sill.

"Blood," he said simply.

Lieutenant Kelly nodded perfunctorily, and turned to me.

"Know how that got there?" he said.

"No. I don't know."

"Did you lean out the window last night?"

I tried to remember, but last night seemed years past, and even my own actions were confused.

"I may have, when I came back upstairs after Mr. Doyle and the doctor left," I said. "I don't remember."

He grunted.

"I want a picture of this," he said to the sergeant.

"O.K., chief."

"Now let's have a look at these bags."

Sergeant Lynch put my luggage up on the bed and opened it. Lieutenant Kelly looked on while he removed the entire contents of both bags. They even opened an empty leather writing case that had got in by accident.

I thought Lieutenant Kelly seemed more interested in it than seemed natural.

"What's that for?" he demanded.

"It usually has small note paper in it," I said. "It's a writing case. My colored maid packed for me. I suppose she thought I might need it, and didn't notice it was empty."

He nodded.

"May I ask what you're hunting for?" I said rather tartly.

He looked rather queerly at me. Then he said, "We'd like to find a thirty-eight automatic revolver for one thing." He winked at Sergeant Lynch.

"You don't mean the gun that killed Mr. Trent?"

"That's the one," he answered amiably.

"Do you mean you haven't found it?"

"That's the idea. Seen it around any place?"

He winked at the sergeant again.

"Why, yes," I said. "I saw it on the table, last night, in front of Mr. Trent."

The mirth disappeared instantly from Lieutenant Kelly's eyes.

"What's that?" he said sharply.

"I said I saw it last night on the table in front of Mr. Trent's body."

"No kidding?"

"Of course not."

"Yeh?" he said. "I guess I want to have a good long talk with you, lady. You just come with me. Keep at it, Bill. Where's Norton?"

"He's doin' the grounds and the garage, chief."

"O.K."

I went downstairs again with Lieutenant Kelly. He took a key out of his pocket and opened the door into the library. The heavy curtains had been pulled aside, but the room seemed cold and dreary. I didn't know that they'd removed Mr. Trent's body, and it was a little shock to see the chair at the table empty. I suppose it would have been a worse one if it had not been.

"Sorry, lady," he said gruffly. "But Doyle said there wasn't any gun in sight last night. Sure you weren't seein' things?"

"No indeed," I said. "When the light went off, I was staring hard at the table and Mr. Trent. I still had an image of it in front of me after the light went off. There was a gun on the table—right here."

I pointed to a spot on the table. There were brown discolored patches where blood had spattered on the mahogany surface.

Lieutenant Kelly took a small but very powerful electric torch out of his pocket and held the beam on the spot. I watched his face as he bent down and looked at it closely from all angles.

"I guess you win, lady," he said after a minute. "There's a little trace of oil there. Lucky you saw that, now; we'd a never run on that by ourselves."

He straightened up and fixed me with a coldly impersonal eye.

"What else do you know about this business, lady? You didn't take that gun, by any chance, now, did you?"

"No. I certainly didn't."

"And you still think somebody turned out the light on you, do you?"

"I certainly do."

He shook his head.

"The fuse blew out, lady. That's what happened."

I looked quickly at him.

"Then there wasn't anybody behind me?"

"Nope."

He pointed to the connection on the floor under the table into which the lamp was plugged. It was covered with a thick brownish stain.

"When Ellicott and Bassett came down," he said, "they couldn't turn on the lights until they'd got a new fuse in. There's blood in the socket. Made a short. We've got the blown fuse."

"Well," I admitted, "I didn't hear anyone, but I could have sworn I heard the click of the switch, not the sort of noise a blown fuse makes."

He seemed to think about it, but he shook his head. "Hard to tell the difference when you're excited," he said.

"Then you don't think there was a gun here either?"

"I wouldn't, if there wasn't that oil there, lady, and that's a fact. And I'm blamed if I see what's the big idea. Both Ellicott and Bassett say there wasn't any here, and they came on the scene at the same time, and a fuse was blown."

He scratched his head.

"It's sure got me beat," he said.

"Do you think, lieutenant," I said with some hesitation, "that somebody else here might be trying to put the blame on Michael Spur?"

He just looked at me.

"You think this is a movie?" he said.

"Well," I replied, "Mr. Trent told me, just a few hours before he was shot, that it was a swell layout for someone if they wanted to use it."

I didn't like the way he'd looked at me, and I replied with some heatedness.

"He did, did he?"

"Yes, he did."

He thought about that for a moment. Then he said, "He didn't just happen to say who'd want to use it, did he?"

"No, he didn't. But I shouldn't think it would be so hard to find out."

I tried to use the same rather scornful tone of voice that he'd used.

"For example, he and Mr. Archer were having a knock-down dragout about this life story of his I was supposed to begin today. And he and Mrs. Trent and Dr. Sartoris were having a set-to earlier in the evening."

At first he listened to me in spite of himself. Then he shook his head.

"It's that red head of yours that's got you going, lady," he said with a grin, and I flushed. My temper *is* pretty short, and my hair *is* rather red, although I prefer having it called Titian.

"And what's more," he went on, lighting another of his poisonous cigars, "what'd you think if I told you Michael Spur came down here to get money to finance this business of making ports in the Near East? And the old man wouldn't give it to him?"

"Who told you that?" I remanded. I was genuinely alarmed.

"That's for me to know, lady," he said, exasperatingly matter-of-fact. "No, all I'm telling you is just keep your shirt on and it'll all come out sooner or later."

He grinned amiably. "No kiddin', now, about that gun? That's straight?"

"Yes."

"O.K. We'll find it. Don't you worry. Now let's go back and find out what the rest of these birds got to say for themselves."

I was a little dampened by all this. I could have sworn I'd heard the click of a switch when that light went off, and I sort of *felt* somebody in the room. I couldn't expect Lieutenant Kelly, of course, to take much stock in anything as vague as all that, so I let it go.

"There's one other thing I wanted to ask you," he said as we went out. "How come you didn't pipe up and tell Spur you saw him over there outside the window at twelve?"

"Oh, dear!" I said. "I forgot."

"Yeah? Well, Mr. Doyle's going to think you never saw him, or you wouldn't have forgot. I'm just telling you, lady—watch your step around here until you find out what it's all about. In fact, I got an idea."

We stopped outside the dining room door.

"You just tell everybody you're thinking of leaving tomorrow—that I said it was O.K. see?"

He slapped his thigh and chuckled heartily.

"I'll explain later," he added.

THIRTEEN

Dr. Sartoris was talking to Mr. Doyle when Lieutenant Kelly and I went back into the dining room.

"I don't want to be misunderstood," he was saying. "This is undoubtedly support of the theory of recurring psychosis, which I advanced. At the same time, Mr. Doyle, I don't want it understood that I *predicted* this occurrence. I didn't. In fact, if I'd thought of Spur's coming back here at the time the subject first came up, I'd never have mentioned it. I was using it as an illustration of the kind of thing that's possible with so-called mental cases."

Lieutenant Kelly broke in.

"You seen Spur today, doctor?" he inquired. "What do you think of him as a mental case now?"

"I talked with him a few minutes last night. I've seen him just casually today. I'm going up shortly to see him."

"All right. Just give us your own statement, then."

Dr. Sartoris, it seemed, had gone upstairs at Mrs. Trent's request to see Michael at eleven o'clock. He had then gone to his room, written a few pages of a lecture he was to give in New York shortly, and had gone to bed and was asleep by midnight, or perhaps a little after. He had heard nothing until he was awakened at two or thereabouts. He knew no reason for anyone's desiring Mr. Trent's death. He had seen the body shortly before Mr. Doyle arrived, in company with Major Ellicott and Perry Bassett. There had been some delay on account of the blown fuse, but the room was orderly, and he agreed with Dr. O'Brien that death had been instantaneous, and was caused by a bullet at very close range. He was, of course, a qualified and practicing doctor of medicine.

After he left us, Perry Bassett was ushered in. I took it that his sister had objected to the brown hat and the old gardening clothes—he was dressed in a dark gray suit and had on a stiff white collar. He looked very respectable and extremely uncomfortable and ill at ease. His story, however, was quite simple. He had gone to bed shortly after eleven, and had been waked by the commotion in the hall. He had given Michael Spur a couple of tablets of phenobarbital, which he himself always took before going to bed, or he'd never get any sleep. Perry Bassett fidgeted and squirmed and tugged at his collar, making the most agonized faces, and finally Lieutenant Kelly let him go.

Agnes Hutton was next. It was the first time I'd seen her all day. She had a large calf-bound edition of the *Contes Drolatiques* under her arm and put it on the table with her handkerchief and a pair of horn-rimmed reading glasses, as if she would like to get back to it as soon as convenient.

She had gone to bed about 11.30. She'd stayed downstairs to talk to Mr. Trent a few moments about some business details, and went directly upstairs when she left him. She had read—she tapped the *Droll Tales* with her forefinger— for a few minutes, and had gone to sleep until she'd heard a noise out in the hall. She thought it was most unfortunate for Michael Spur—in fact she blamed herself definitely, because Mrs. Trent had remarked in Michael's presence at the bridge table that she hoped the gun in the library table wasn't loaded, and she had told Michael she would move it somewhere else. When she went to the library Mr. Trent had told her to get some papers and go over them with him, and the other matter had slipped her mind.

"As a matter of fact, though," she said, "I wasn't much worried about it. I thought it was a lot of nonsense. Michael looked better than I'd ever seen him."

Major Ellicott had gone upstairs shortly after eleven. He was manager of the estate, and also had an interest in the business of Trent and Spur. The day's bills were always left on his desk, and he filed them himself at night before he went to bed. Last night he was dog-tired, and he'd taken a stiff shot of whiskey and gone to bed. He had slept until wakened at two. He assumed the reason he hadn't heard the shot was that his room was across the corridor over the dining room, while Miss Cather's, who had heard it, was directly over the library itself.

Cheryl was next, and she had nothing to add, except that she didn't think Michael had anything to do with it. I waited for her to say Agnes Hutton did it, but she didn't. I was very glad when she got out of the room.

Mr. Doyle left for town a little later, and Lieutenant

Kelly said he wouldn't need me any longer. He was going to have a talk with the servants.

"Remember to tell 'em I said you could go tomorrow," he said.

So I announced it quite casually, I thought, at lunch, to which everybody showed up except Mrs. Trent, Cheryl and Michael Spur.

Agnes Hutton wanted to know how I'd worked it, and Major Ellicott shook his head at her.

"You aren't going to run out on us, Agnes, are you?" he protested. "There's an awful lot of work to be done around here, and you're the only person that knows very much about it."

Agnes smiled her mocking smile.

"I've been most definitely asked to leave," she said silkily. "Mrs. Trent very clearly said the sooner the better. You know, I don't think she likes me very much."

"You're not just finding that out, Agnes?" Mr. Archer inquired, his blue eyes twinkling unexpectedly. "I imagine if we all left because Emily doesn't like us, there'd have been a traffic congestion at the gate this morning. In fact, Sartoris here is about the only one who'd have stayed on."

Dr. Sartoris smiled tolerantly. He apparently didn't mind being twitted about Mrs. Trent. Perry Bassett seemed to be the only one who did mind it, but he concentrated on the crisp brown crab cakes in front of him, and said nothing.

After lunch he asked me if I'd like to see the place. He seemed to be hunting for an excuse to get out of the house.

"My sister feels it's disrespectful of me to work outside just now," he explained once, when he glanced behind him and surreptitiously dived after a tiny weed that had sprung up in a strawberry forcing bed we were looking at.

We wandered through an elaborate series of formal gardens off to one side of the house until we came to a long row of Lombardy poplars just coming into greenish yellow leaf. At the end of the poplar walk there was a terrace, and beyond it, as far as the eye could reach, there was a sloping wilderness of white waxy dogwood in glorious bloom. And in and out of it were great patches of magenta Judas Tree. It was so lovely it fairly took my breath away.

"Duncan planted all that," he said simply. "But Emily doesn't like it. Do you ride?"

I said yes, and he said, "You must get Cheryl to take you out in the morning. I hope you won't go away. In fact, I don't think it's true that you are going. Did that man tell you to say you were going just to see what would happen?"

I tried not to look as flabbergasted as I felt.

"What makes you think that?" I asked.

"That's what I would do if I were in his place," he replied. "There's twenty-five miles of bridle path through the dogwood. It goes down to an inlet. That's where we swim."

For the remainder of our walk Perry Bassett adroitly side-stepped my rather fumbling attempts to get him to tell what he really thought about Michael Spur and the gruesome business of the previous night. I did learn quite a lot about the best kind of fertilizer for Maryland soil, but I've forgotten it all now. I had the idea several times that this mild pleasant old fellow, who came just to my nose, was making it all up as he went along. But I wasn't sure.

When we came back to the house Lieutenant Kelly was standing on the other side of Perry's flaming crescent of varicolored tulips, looking up at the window. I noticed with a start that Sergeant Lynch was leaning out of the window in my room.

I glanced at Perry Bassett. He had seen them too.

"I wish he'd walk around things," he said, when Lieutenant Kelly sprang across one end of the crescent in what seemed to me a very creditable standing broad jump. He appeared to be in a hurry to meet the uniformed messenger boy whom old Magothy was conducting through the door into the garden. We saw him open several envelopes and skim hastily through the messages. When he saw us he folded them all up and put them in his coat pocket, and beckoned to us.

"Oh, dear!" said Perry Bassett, looking around him for a way out. "You tell him to excuse me. I've got to see a . . . a man."

"About a dog, I suppose," I said.

"No, no. It's about something else."

Lieutenant Kelly grinned at me. He seemed in rather better spirits than he had been before lunch. I was wondering if he'd got something important out of the servants, but he settled that at once.

"Only four of 'em live in the house," he said, "and the old fellow heard the shot and locked all the doors of the servants' quarters until Bassett routed him out hunting for a fuse."

I told him what Perry Bassett had so calmly said about my leaving. He got quite sober, and said "Too bad."

Sergeant Lynch was still looking out of my window, but Lieutenant Kelly didn't seem to feel any explanation was necessary. He merely nodded to the sergeant and came in the house with me.

"I'd like a talk with you if you've got time," he said. We went into the dining room and he closed the door. "Sit down," he said.

He took three telegrams out of his pocket and looked them over. Then he handed one to me. I gasped a little when I saw it was signed by one Harvey McCrea.

LOUISE CATHER COMMISSIONED TO WRITE LIFE STORY OF DUNCAN TRENT STOP LEFT NEW YORK MONDAY 2.10 STOP WEARING BROWN TWEED SUIT BROWN HAT BROWN SHOES STOP RED HAIR YELLOW GREENISH EYES TWENTY EIGHT YEARS OLD STOP HAS WHISKEY CONTRALTO VOICE STOP SMOKES CONSTANTLY STOP WILL FURNISH BAIL IF NECESSARY

I read it a second time. Lieutenant Kelly was watching me through his white eyelashes, grinning.

"Guess you're all right," he said.

"Did you doubt it?"

"Always doubt everything," he said, handing me a second telegram. It was from Santa Rey, Arizona.

MICHAEL SPUR EMPLOYED ASSISTANT CHIEF ENGINEER SANTA REY CONSTRUCTION COMPANY LEFT APRIL SEVENTEENTH DESTINATION NEW YORK NO RECORD UNUSUAL ILLNESS WHILE HERE STOP RESIDENCE SANTA REY HOTEL SIX YEARS MANAGER REPORTS SPUR QUIET AND SOBER STOP NO RECORD OF SLEEPWALKING STOP LOCAL DOCTOR TREATED SPUR FOR SNAKE BITE 1928 ALSO COLD 1929 STOP NO FRIENDS KNOWN OUTSIDE CONSTRUCTION COMPANY STOP YOUNG DARK WOMAN VISITED SANTA REY DECEMBER STOP SPUR ACCOMPANIED HER LOS ANGELES STOP GONE ONE WEEK STOP NO CORRESPONDENCE RECEIVED HERE STOP COMPANY KNOWS NOTHING ABOUT PREVIOUS LIFE STOP EMPLOYED AS DRAUGHTSMAN ON RECOMMENDATION DEPARTMENT OF ENGINEERING UNIVERSITY OF CALIFORNIA SEPTEMBER 1927 PROMOTED ASSISTANT CHIEF 1929 STOP PRESENT ADDRESS HOTEL VANDERBILT NEW YORK CITY

It was signed "Moxon, Chief of Police, Santa Rey."

"Am I supposed to be the dark woman," I asked, "who took him to Los Angeles?"

Lieutenant Kelly ignored my question and handed me a third telegram. It was from the dean of the college of engineering at the U. of C.

MICHAEL SPUR SPLENDID RECORD HERE NINETEEN TWENTYONE TO TWENTYFIVE NO RECORD OF NERVOUS DISTURBANCE STOP INFIRMARY RECORD SHOW ADMISSION MAY NINETEEN TWENTY TWO STOP TREATED FOR SPRAINED BACK STOP ROWED THREE VARSITY CREW STOP NO RECORD OF SLEEPWALKING STOP

I handed it back to Lieutenant Kelly.

"Well," I said, "where does that get us?"

He put it with a fourth message that he hadn't shown me, and put the lot of them back in his pocket.

"Well," he said, "now, it practically lets you out of it."

"No!" I said.

"Yeh. And it puts the last crimp in somebody's bright idea about a psychosis, or whatever they call 'em. Old man Trent was murdered, lady, and he was murdered in cold blood, what's more. When I came down here I thought I knew what for. I ain't so sure just now. There's something funny going on round here."

"I've missed it, if there is," I said. "Do you still want me to pack and pretend I'm leaving?"

"You might as well. Tomorrow after lunch's the time," he said. "I got a man working in Baltimore, and I guess I'd be glad if you'd keep an eye peeled and let me know if you find out anything around here. I'd appreciate it."

"I've found out several things, Lieutenant Kelly," I said. "But I don't know how much I ought to tell you."

He nodded.

"Yeh, I know. But I'm going to find it all out sooner or later. It don't do no good holdin' out on me."

"Then I'll tell you something about the first night I was here," I said. It was hard to realize that "the first night I was here" was just last night.

I told him about seeing Michael come and stop down at the bench where his father had dropped, dead, when he was shot. I told him about hearing Agnes Hutton saying that if I was as smart as I thought I was it was a rotten time to have me around.

He was much more interested in that than he was in Michael's actions.

"You don't know who she was talkin' to?"

"No. I didn't hear him speak, really. I just heard a sort of mumble. But I heard Agnes say he needn't make love to her."

He thought about that a moment. Then he asked me why I'd happened to come to Ivy Hill—who'd suggested Mr. Trent as a subject for the magazine, who'd made the arrangements, and so on. I told him I didn't know, but I thought McCrae had met Mr. Trent at a dinner at the Maryland Club.

"I guess I can find out about all that," he said.

He pulled out a bilious-colored gold-mounted fountain pen and began jotting things down.

"I guess it boils down to this, lady," he said meditatively. "Either Spur's off his nut and did it without knowing it, or he did it premeditated, or somebody else did it and's tryin' to make Spur take the rap. Now, we'll just call them one, two and three. *And* we'll just let Number One go."

He screwed the top back on his fountain pen. I thought it was obvious that he didn't feel particularly at home on paper. He thrust his hands in his trousers pockets and slouched down in his chair.

"Now take Number Two. If Spur did it, and is tryin' to get out of it by play-actin', then my idea when I came down here is all wrong. And I got to find a motive that fits *him*. But if you take Number Three, then my idea's all right. And if Number Three's right, then I got to find a motive that'll fit: one, Agnes Hutton; two, Major Ellicott; three, Archer; four, Dr. Sartoris; or five, the old woman."

"Are you being mysterious, or have you got a reason for keeping your swell idea to yourself?" I asked.

He grinned.

"I'll just hang onto it for a while," he said blandly, getting up. "Mind you don't say nothing about it. We'll, I got work to do."

He looked at his watch.

"I'll be seein' you, lady. Can you get them notes typed out for me?"

When I was sitting a little later on a stool in front of my typewriter, I got to wondering about the things I hadn't told Lieutenant Kelly, and wondering what sort of theory Dr. Sartoris would trot out of the psychoanalytic paddock to fit my omissions. I counted them up. First, I hadn't told him about Cheryl and Michael and the spear. Not that that proved anything, but it certainly added more brick to the wall that Lieutenant Kelly was building around Michael Spur. The meaning of the telegrams from the West was plain enough.

Second, I hadn't told him about the telegram that dropped out of Dr. Sartoris's pocket on the train. Third, that Dr. Sartoris had subsequently denied knowledge of Michael's return. Fourth, that Mrs. Trent had pretended she hadn't been waiting for him all day. Fifth, that Mrs. Trent was planning to buy the Foster place for Dr. Sartoris.

In fact, as I thought about it, it seemed to me very much as if I'd done my best to shield a man who I was convinced was a pretty detestable sort of person. I hadn't even the satisfaction of being able to tell myself I'd done it to protect a silly old woman from the consequences of her own folly.

I was finishing Michael's statement, and had put another sheet of paper in my typewriter, when I heard a commotion outside. I went over to my window and looked out.

Lieutenant Kelly was standing on the far side of the bed of tulips. But it wasn't really a bed of tulips any longer. There were three men down there, armed with spades, and they were digging it up, systematically. I looked on, perfectly horrified, at the wanton destruction. Suddenly one of the men shouted, and they all dropped their spades and watched, while he bent over and picked something up out of the hole he'd made in the bed. He held it out to Lieutenant Kelly. It was covered with moist soil, but I could see that it was a revolver.

It seemed, I learned later on, that the business of finding the gun buried in the tulip bed was a simple piece of two-plus-two logic on Lieutenant Kelly's part. The blood on my window ledge indicated that somebody who'd been in contact with the murdered man had been there. There was no evidence on the tile trimming outside that anyone had gone out my window; there must have been some other point, then, in the blood there. Lieutenant Kelly had concluded also that odd and casual as Perry Bassett was, he wasn't enough so to spend the morning weeding in the garden, at that particular spot, while his brother-in-law was lying in the welter of his own drying blood in the library a hundred feet away.

Personally I should have said Perry Bassett was remote enough from life to do almost anything, but in this instance Lieutenant Kelly was right, when he had concluded that Perry or somebody had thrown something from my window down into the tulip bed and Perry had buried it there.

He wrapped the gun up and sent it to Baltimore by a state

policeman, and poor Perry Bassett was summoned into the dining room.

I went to see Cheryl and told her as much as I'd seen from my window—that the gun had been found in the tulip bed and that Sergeant Lynch had been sent to bring Perry for examination. She was sitting crosslegged on the floor taping a tennis racket when I came in, and didn't seem in the least perturbed by the news.

"What on earth do you suppose the silly did that for?" she asked, in a slightly puzzled tone.

"I suppose he really had to find the gun," I suggested ironically.

"No, I mean Perry," she said seriously. "Why did he put it there, of all places?"

For a moment I had a sneaking feeling that Cheryl was in some respects her mother's daughter after all.

"You see, you don't know Perry," she went on, as if she'd guessed part of what I was thinking. "He's very curious, and if he hid it there, he must have had something in mind. Don't make the mistake that Perry had anything to do with it," she added. "He couldn't hurt anything. There's a family of jackrabbits that eat all the vegetables he grows every year, and we have to get other vegetables from the next farm, because he won't have them killed."

I was forced to admit there was something very fine in Cheryl's conviction, in the face of obvious evidence, that the people she liked couldn't do things she didn't like. So I said, "Well, I hope Lieutenant Kelly sees it that way."

FOURTEEN

Oddly enough, it seemed that Lieutenant Kelly did see it exactly that way. At least, that's the impression he gave Perry. I ran into Perry when I went downstairs a little early to read the papers before dinner. He was sitting on the terrace outside the open windows of the living room, his back turned on the ravished remains of his tulip bed. He had a big leather-bound seed catalogue on his knees, and he was staring sadly at it. So far as I know it was his only form of literary indulgence. At least it was the only thing I ever saw him read, just as the *Contes Drolatiques* that Agnes Hutton carried about was the only book I ever saw her with. The seed catalogue was opened at a spread of gorgeous deep-hued peonies, the sort that are never seen on land or sea or anywhere except in seed catalogues. He looked around like a startled rabbit when he heard me coming. Then he smiled nervously and cleared his throat.

"I made a mistake," he said simply.

"You did?" I said. "How?"

"Well, that man in there (which was the only way he ever referred to Lieutenant Kelly) says I was foolish to try to hide the gun, because it began to look like my brother-in-law killed himself. The gun was right by his hand, and he said the shot was fired very close, so it could have been, you see."

"Why did you hide it?" I asked.

"Oh," he said meekly, "I guess I lost my head. "You see, I heard the shot. I went downstairs, and you were already there, in front of me. Of course, I knew what had happened, and I didn't want the police to get the gun, with Michael's fingerprints on it. I turned out the light."

He looked timidly at me and blinked guiltily.

"I guess I scared you?"

"I guess you did too," I said.

"Then you ran through the library, and I got the gun in the dark, and that's how I got the blood all over me. Anyway, while you were getting back through the back staircase, I got upstairs. Your door was open, and I had the gun, so I just dived in and threw it out the window and got back to my room just as you came up."

I was a little startled.

"Who blew out the fuse, then?" I demanded.

He glanced around cautiously, and beckoned me closer.

"That's the funny thing," he said. "Somebody was in the library between the time you and I left and the time Dick Ellicott and I went down."

"Who do you think it was?"

"That's what that man in there asked me, but I don't know. All I know is that it was me that turned out the light and me that got the gun. I'm sorry I did, because if Mr. Doyle could think it was suicide everything would have been all right."

I was a little disappointed in his attitude, because Mr. Trent had seemed rather fond of him.

"Aren't you a little sorry Mr. Trent's dead?" I said.

"Oh, yes. I am sorry in some ways," he said frankly. "He let me stay here after I lost all my money, but he wasn't constructive. I mean he wouldn't do anything to really get me started again. You know"—he glanced over his shoulder again, and lowered his voice, which was already in the stage-whisper class—"I'll tell you all about it sometime. If I had ten thousand dollars right now, or next week even, I could clean up on Wall Street. There's absolutely not a chance to lose."

He shook his head sadly.

"But Duncan wouldn't help me out. Then he was cross to my sister lots of times. But Emily is a little foolish. You haven't noticed it so soon, but she does very odd things for a woman of her age. You know, flowers don't ever get as big as the ones they have pictures of."

I glanced around. No one was in sight, but a minute later Dr. Sartoris appeared in the window and came outside. Magothy followed with a tray of cocktails. He had a large black crêpe heart sewed to the sleeve of his white coat.

Dr. Sartoris said "Good evening" and sat down. I don't know whether he knew about the revolver or not. He asked quite casually if the police had dug up the tulip bed. Perry looked around and winced at the sight, and I said yes, they had.

"I hear there's a possibility of suicide," he said. "In 'fact Mr. Doyle telephoned Mrs. Trent and said they were discussing it. Have you seen Lieutenant Kelly since then?"

I hadn't seen him since I'd looked out of my window and seen him directing the tulip bed operations. I did, however, know that he'd spent some time in the library with Mr. Archer and Agnes Hutton and Major Ellicott. I knew also that he had run into town and brought Mr. Doyle out to Ivy Hill. The two of them had talked with Mr. Archer and Agnes, and Mr. Doyle had gone back to town.

At 7:30, while we were sitting out on the terrace still, Magothy came out to announce dinner, and said that Mr. Archer and Agnes would not be with us; they were still in the library with Lieutenant Kelly. Later we heard that Kelly had gone to Baltimore. Everybody seemed to breathe a little easier. Agnes and Mr. Archer joined us, Cheryl came down with her mother. Mrs. Trent was dressed in a flowing black lace Lanvin with long skintight sleeves and no back to speak of. The change in her was positively startling. She ignored Mr. Archer and Major Ellicott with the aplomb of a Hollywood duchess, and leaned on Dr. Sartoris, mentally and physically, with the coyness of a Broadway ingénue with a Park Avenue apartment.

It was Victor this, and Victor that, and Victor will you ask Magothy to turn off the radio, when Major Ellicott was reading the paper within two feet of it. She made no allusion to Mr. Doyle's suicide theory. In fact, outside of a sort of subdued languor, there was not the slightest reason to think she was not a very contented woman. When she and Dr. Sartoris strolled out into the moonlight—it was Mrs. Trent's idea, she hadn't had a breath of air all day—there was a positive collapse in the atmosphere. Mr. Archer bid two spades with me holding three honors and two outside aces. As I was his partner we lost only two on our seven bid. Major Ellicott threw his paper on the floor and got up.

"How about a little billiards, Michael?" he said, and they went out, taking Agnes Hutton with them.

Cheryl and Perry were both intent on their hands. She had remarkable control, but I'd discovered that when her eyes were widest, and her face had a sort of plastic woodenness, she was the most intensely aware of things. I avoided looking at her when major Ellicott came back into the living room and said something about three being a crowd. Nobody at the bridge table paid any attention to him, except possibly Perry Bassett, who went down four doubled, redoubled and vulnerable. But he was likely to do that any time.

Dr. Sartoris and Mrs. Trent were still out when Mr. Archer announced, rather testily, that he was going to bed. Cheryl moved her chair back, saying she'd have to pay me in the morning—twenty-eight cents, I think we'd won—and strolled over to Major Ellicott. He looked up at her and smiled.

"I'm tired, Dick," she said.

"You'd better get off to bed, dear."

"I want to talk to you a few minutes. Can't we go outside?"

"You'll take cold, Cheryl," Perry protested. He was counting out twenty-eight cents to Mr. Archer.

I said good night and went upstairs. I met Agnes Hutton on the landing and we went up together.

"Sleepy?" she said.

"No."

"Come in and have a cigarette with me."

I went in with her. Her room was just like mine, except that she had an efficient-looking table with a typewriter on it in front of one window.

She tossed the book she was carrying—it was the same copy of the *Contes Drolatiques*—on the bed and dropped into a chair by the fireplace.

"What time are you going tomorrow?" she asked abruptly.

"After lunch," I replied.

She didn't say anything for a few moments. Then she said, "Would you do something for me?"

I hesitated.

She shrugged her slim shoulders and raised one corner of her carefully rouged mouth in a sardonic little smile.

"Sounds odd, doesn't it?" she said. "But I can't explain exactly. I'll tell you this much—I'm up to my neck in something I wish I was out of. It looks like I'm welshing at the last minute. Well, I guess that's what I am doing."

"Look here, Miss Hutton," I said. "Don't tell me anything you don't want Lieutenant Kelly to know, because I promised I'd tell him anything I heard—that might help him find out who murdered Mr. Trent."

She laughed, and it wasn't a very pleasant sound.

"I didn't shoot Mr. Trent," she said coolly. "And that's why I want to get away from here. Have you heard about his will?"

"No."

"You will soon. Dick Ellicott and Archer are joint trustees

102

with Mrs. Trent. She gets a third of the estate, in cash, bonds and so on. Cheryl gets the rest of it, free of all restrictions on her twenty-first birthday."

"Isn't that what everybody expected?"

"Yes—but Michael Spur's back. And Michael Spur's money doesn't exist any more, except on paper. And paper doesn't amount to much right now. Trent and Spur stock is off the market—they dropped it when it got to one and three-quarters. In nineteen-twenty-eight it was two hundred fifteen. Michael owns nine-tenths of the stock. He bought everybody else's stock at two hundred—especially Mr. Trent's."

"Does he know it?"

"Yes. I told him."

"When?"

"Last Christmas. When I was visiting in Bermuda."

"Bermuda?"

"Oh, Arizona, then."

She laughed again, much the same way as before.

"You know, I was in love with Michael for a long time. I even hated him for a long time until Victor showed me that was just another form of being in love with him. So I snapped out of it. I'm rather sorry for him, now. That's why I've got to get out—I know too much about all this. And I want you to do something for me."

"What is it?" I said practically.

"If you won't do it, will you regard it as between you and me?"

"Yes."

"All right. I want you to take a few things to New York for me when you go tomorrow. This book and a few things I'll leave in the top drawer of that dresser. I'll be there as quick as you are."

She leaned forward, and all her mocking superior manner was gone. I saw her as I knew she was, an intelligent, level-headed woman who'd got caught between the millstones of a thwarted emotional life. I didn't feel sorry for her. She wasn't that sort.

"If you'll do that for me, Louise Cather, I'll be very glad," she said in a low voice, as if she thought someone might be listening to her. "I didn't kill Mr. Trent. That's top level, as Michael says. But I've got to get out, that's all."

"All right," I said. "I'll do that. If I don't get away tomorrow, I'll bring them when I come. Is that all right?"

She hesitated a moment.

"Yes. That's all right. Give me your New York phone number. If I don't get you there, I'll phone you here tomorrow night."

I gave her my number and she went with me to the door. Dr. Sartoris was just coming out of Michael Spur's room. I was surprised to see his face. The amused confident diagnosing expression was gone; he looked like a man who was genuinely troubled about something.

When he saw us, he was immediately himself again, though he was rather cool to me. "Perhaps you can tell me something, Miss Hutton," he said. I left them standing in the hall and went into my own room. Several times in the next hour I thought of going back and telling Agnes that I'd changed my mind and that probably Lieutenant Kelly wasn't going to let me go tomorrow. But I didn't. I plastered my face with some cold cream out of a very exotic looking jar in the bathroom, wiped it off and went to bed. I didn't wake up until Aspasia knocked at my door and said Miss Cheryl was riding for an hour before breakfast and would I like to join her.

Cheryl and Major Ellicott were waiting for me with a sleek beautifully poised chestnut mare, and we started out, Cheryl in the lead. She was headed for the poplar lane shimmering across the gardens in the early morning sun.

"Let's take Miss Cather down by the golf course, Cheryl," Major Ellicott suggested. But Cheryl said she wanted to go down to the beach.

"You're the general," said Major Ellicott, and we continued along the drive until Cheryl turned by the little lake near the gate. The black swan swam quickly to the edge of the pool—it was what the English would call an "ornamental water"—and gobbled up the bread Cheryl threw him. She was in much lighter spirits than I'd seen her before, and she cantered ahead and waited for Major Ellicott and me with our more leisurely pace.

It was a heavenly morning as we rode through the poplar lane, Major Ellicott pointing out various things he wanted to do with the place. At last we came into view of the dogwood and Judas Tree. My mare picked her way down the steep terrace, and we entered a sort of fairyland of waxen and magenta blossoms, cool and fragrant as they brushed my cheeks. I was still ahead of Major Ellicott. Cheryl had disappeared entirely. I was leaning back to listen to Major Ellicott telling me about Mr. Trent's passion for dogwood, and how they always came here in the spring no matter what happened—when suddenly from somewhere in the snowy distance there came a high blood-curdling scream. I dug my heels into the mare, and she burst into a gallop. Major Ellicott was behind me, pressing to take the lead as the path through the woods widened. But he didn't make it. We turned sharply into a small clearing, and I saw Cheryl half standing in the stirrups, her reins taut, her horse backing from something in front of him. I got to her before Major Ellicott did—and I saw it, just as my mare jerked back from the horrible thing in front of us.

It was Agnes Hutton. Her body was hanging from an old-fashioned lamp post behind a rustic bench that stood by a little stream running through the open space in the woods. Her head was tilted at an unbelievable angle above the knotted rope, and her body looked as if it were resting against a solid bed of the white dogwood. Her right hand, clutching desperately in the very moment of violent death, had caught a branch of magenta Judas Tree. The feathery blossoms bruised and blackened in her clenched stiffening hand. Her face was purple and distorted; she looked as though she had been frozen with horror.

FIFTEEN

Cheryl and I dashed out of that ghastly rendezvous at full gallop, our heads ducked to protect our faces from the sharp stinging slaps of the dogwood blossoms along the narrow path. My mind groped desperately to remember something in our talk the night before that might explain the terrible distorted figure back there. And nothing would come except the image of those few shocked seconds, the dogwood, the leaden swaying body, the rigid white hand clutching the red branch of death. I'd taken it all in, even the grass beneath, blue with late violets, her dark blue straw turban, her gloves lying in the middle of the rustic bridge across the brook, as if she had been snatched back to her death while she was fleeing. From something she had feared? I hadn't thought that the night before. I hadn't thought of fear as having anything to do with it—it seemed just a sort of nostalgia, the modern form of remorse. Getting out because it was the thing to do. Then I wondered how early she'd gone—and I thought of something else, and dug my heels in the mare's side and literally flew, wanting, desperately, to keep my faith with Agnes Hutton. If I could get there before someone else got there and got the things she wanted me to take to New York for her!

My horse and Cheryl's behind me pounded down the drive, and Magothy, with a blue apron round his stomach, sweeping the paved entry to the big hall, stopped broom in hand and stared at us as if we were the hosts of the damned descending on him.

"Get Mr. Perry, Magothy!" Cheryl gasped, but before the old Negro could move we were both off our horses and in the house. "You phone the police, Louise, and I'll get Perry and Victor. Oh, why isn't Lieutenant Kelly here!"

I ran into the library and picked up the phone, and waited interminably for the languid "Number, please," and then interminably until I heard Mr. Doyle's voice. I told him, and told him also that Lieutenant Kelly wasn't out yet, and hung up. In the hall people were coming downstairs, talking excitedly, rushing about, collecting in circles. I could hear Mrs. Trent say it was just like Agnes Hutton to do something of the sort when we already had trouble and to spare.

I slipped to the other end of the library and up the stairs in the family wing. No one was in sight. I ran quickly to Agnes' room and opened the door. Her bed was rumpled up but it hadn't been seriously slept in, and her yellow silk nightdress was crumpled just enough to deceive a colored maid who didn't care anyway. Otherwise the room looked the same as it had the night before.

I went quickly to the dresser drawer, thinking it was lucky I had my riding gloves still on, and opened it. There was a little bundle of papers there, and several pads that looked like shorthand notebooks, all fastened together with a wide rubber band. I took them out and started back across the room to get the book. The window was open, and I heard Mr. Archer's voice from outside: "Lock up her room until the police get here."

I made a dash for the door, and got into my room just as Mrs. Trent, coming upstairs, said, "Give me the key, Magothy, I'll lock the door. You go see about breakfast. We can't all go round on empty stomachs all day."

I stuffed Agnes's bundle of papers between the mattress and the rope springs of Queen Elizabeth's and my bed, and rushed downstairs again. Somehow I felt a lot safer. Everybody was gone, and I started out too, and stopped, thinking someone ought to be there at the house when Mr. Doyle came. I was standing there in the drive when Magothy came out and said my breakfast was on the table out on the dining room terrace if I'd like to have it. That's where I was, eating popovers and honey and thinking as hard as I could, but without much point, when a Ford coupé rattled up and Lieutenant Kelly got out, resplendent in a very light gray suit, a crushed raspberry shirt and stiff collar, a green tie, and with a green silk handkerchief in his breast pocket. It seemed almost a shame to tell him there was another murder. It was obvious he didn't know it—he looked too pleased with himself and his get-up and life generally.

It's curious now to remember that I ran out and told him what had happened. I could almost swear he was as stunned by the news as we had been by the fact. But his recovery was instantaneous. Sergeant Lynch was with him in the car, and he rapped out orders to him to stay at the house, lock Miss Hutton's door, watch everything and move nothing.

"Now, then, lady!" he said, and together we ran—at least he ran, as easily as if he'd been in training for a marathon, and I fell out at the poplar alley, not being used to that sort of thing. That's why everything was over when I got there. Anyway, it's not easy to run in riding boots.

Major Ellicott had cut the rope and laid the body of Agnes Hutton on the grass. "Couldn't stand seeing her hanging there like that," he said later to Dr. O'Brien. Dr. Sartoris had pronounced her dead when he'd got there, and when Dr. O'Brien got there the two of them agreed that she had been dead not much longer than three hours. It was then a little after seven. What she had been doing there, a mile from the house, at four o'clock in the morning was a natural question. Her hat and gloves, and her bag with $55.00 in cash and a check book on a New York bank seemed conclusive evidence that she was leaving Ivy Hill on short notice.

So much was evident and not much more. Our horses' hoofs and Dick Ellicott's and Dr. Sartoris's footprints had trodden the violet-carpeted turf into an effective mess. Lieutenant Kelly ordered everybody back to the house. I glanced at them while they were leaving. Mr. Archer was still in his pajamas and dressing gown. Perry had flakes of dried lather around his ears and under his nose. One side of his face was shaved and the other was not, so that he looked ridiculously like one of those before and after using ads for razor blades.

Michael Spur was partly dressed, and there was something new about him—he looked as if something had snapped and liberated him again, at least partly. I glanced at Cheryl, slim and straight in her white linen riding breeches and black boots and thin white turtle-neck sweater, her hair a living gold in the morning sun, her wide eyes the color of the purple iris just beginning to bloom along the sheltered sunny banks of the little brook. She was watching Michael, and when Major Ellicott put his arm around her shoulders to lead her away I thought she looked a little startled, as if she hadn't expected it. I was rather startled myself when Dr. Sartoris said, "Let's call a truce, Miss Cather. I want to talk to you."

I looked up at him. His face was a little pale under the blond stubble of his morning's beard, and his eyes were so deadly serious that I felt a little shiver go down my spine.

I turned to follow the rest. Just then Lieutenant Kelly barked at me, "I'll want you a minute!" I said, "Later, Dr.

Sartoris," and he bowed. Manners, I thought, are rather ridiculous when you're not shaved and your pajamas have been slept in. And that struck me as rather odd.

"Dr. Sartoris's pajamas were perfectly fresh at two o'clock the other night," I said to Lieutenant Kelly.

"The Hutton woman already told me that," he snapped. After that I kept quiet.

It seems that all he wanted me there for was to order me, very brusquely, not to talk to anybody until I'd talked to him. I have an unfortunate impulse to sudden anger, and I felt myself flaring up, and he felt it too. He shot out his hand and seized my wrist in a grip of steel.

"Don't be a fool, lady," he said. "Look here."

He let go my wrist and took a telegram out of his pocket. He thrust it at me. I saw in a flash that it was the same as the one that had fallen from Dr. Sartoris's pocket on the train.

MICHAEL SPUR RETURNING URGENT
COME AT ONCE LOVE EMILY TRENT

I looked blankly at him. All my wrath had vanished—as it always does—into thin air.

"You knew about that?" he demanded.

I nodded.

He handed me another one. It was signed "Agnes Hutton" and it made a reservation on the *Europa* sailing at midnight Friday.

"Know the point about them two telegrams?" he said.

"No."

"Well, it's this—they were both sent by the same woman. Mrs. Trent never sent that. Agnes Hutton sent 'em both. She's well known in town, they remembered her."

I stared at him. When he spoke next his voice was not so rough.

"You get the idea? That's why I'm telling you to be careful, lady. There's a killer around here—there's one of these good friends of yours wouldn't stop a minute to treat you like that."

He waved his hand casually up at the lamp post.

"So don't you talk—see? You watch yourself. All right, now. You run along and finish your breakfast."

SIXTEEN

I won't go into the details of the morning. Some of them were rather painful, especially the one dealing with the large raw spot on my heel where my riding boots, not used to two-mile hikes, had rubbed. While I was upstairs swabbing it with mercurochrome, Aspasia came in and told me that Lieutenant Kelly and Mr. Doyle and the other man—I supposed it was Sergeant Lynch—had got the key to Agnes Hutton's room from Mrs. Trent and were in there. Also that they'd phoned for a lot of men from Baltimore and Heaven knows what more.

It wasn't until almost eleven that they called on me to help them take everybody's statement. Before that I'd seen Michael and Mrs. Trent.

Mrs. Trent, in fact, had sent Aspasia for me, and I hobbled down to her room in one shoe and one black satin mule. She opened the door for me and said, "Come in, Miss Mather, and sit down. I want you to do something for me. That's a mighty cute dress you've got on. What an odd design!"

The design, which I noticed for the first time, was a large splotch of mercurochrome on the right knee of a simple white crêpe dress.

"I'll be glad to, Mrs. Trent," I said, "if I can."

She looked blank. "Oh, it isn't at all hard," she said.

I sat down and waited.

"They're going to have the funeral today," she went on. The complacent tone of her voice was almost horrible. I don't really believe that she had actually realized what she was saying or how it sounded to other people.

"You can go in town with us, and then step up to Mr. Murchison's office and tell him I'll pay anything that's necessary to get the Foster place. Do you hear? *Anything at all.*"

"Don't you think it would be better if Major Ellicott or Mr. Archer looked after that for you, Mrs. Trent?"

"Why, of all the impudence!" said Mrs. Trent. "I never in my life!"

Then, realizing, I suppose, that I was neither her servant nor her daughter, she immediately made an about-face.

"No, no," she said, in a cajoling tone. "I'll tell you. It's this way. They don't understand. You see, it's to be a sanatorium for Dr. Sartoris, a gift from me and my late husband for the advancement of psychology. Victor doesn't think it's a good idea."

I was a little surprised at that; I should have thought he would think it a fine idea.

"Why not?" I said.

"Well, he thinks it's a little out of the way."

She shifted her bulk against the multicolored cushions on the yellow satin chaise longue.

"He really wants to be in New York. I promised him a hundred and fifty thousand dollars to build himself a hospital, but of course if I can get the Foster place for about thirty or forty thousand, it'll be that much to the good."

"Naturally," I said.

"And it's near Ivy Hill."

She was not cajoling now, or simpering; it was just a good practical scheme for keeping him near her.

"Of course Victor says that's a very great inducement."

Of course he did. I could hear him. I writhed a little, uneasily.

"But anyway, it's best not to say anything about it to anybody—not even Victor—until it's all ready, and I can have the deed all made over and put it on his breakfast tray some morning. Is that an idea?"

"It certainly is," I said.

"Well, that's all, then. You take care of it for me, and I'll see you again before you go. Do you think I ought to arrange to give you power of attorney?"

"No," I said flatly.

"Maybe it won't be necessary."

She started humming something gay.

I thought I'd make one last conscientious attempt to dissuade her before I did anything else about it. I said, "Have you thought, Mrs. Trent, that maybe Dr. Sartoris feels he's too close to the Baltimore medical centers, and hence that this isn't a good place for a sanatorium?"

"Nonsense!" she said quite tartly. "Victor will do as I say, and don't you worry about *that*."

The only thing that did make me worry about it, a little,

was Cheryl's chance remark that her father had said they couldn't afford it. It seemed a strange sort of business altogether. However, I supposed it was Mrs. Trent's affair.

As I was going back to my room Mr. Doyle came out of Agnes's room, and I stopped him.

"Do you know anything about the Foster property?" I asked.

He was obviously thinking about other things, but he managed a smile.

"Thinking of buying it?" he said. "Well don't—because it'll probably run up to thirty thousand, and it'll cost you that much again to put it in shape. They call it Foster's Folly, and they're right."

"Thanks," I said.

"By the way," he went on, "can you help us out again, in about an hour?"

"I'll be glad to."

He locked Agnes's door and I went into my own room. At first I thought I'd got in the wrong place. Michael Spur was sitting there in front of the window, staring out.

"Hullo," I said. "Anything wrong?"

"Haven't you heard, for God's sake?" he said.

"Plenty," I replied. "I thought there might be something else."

It was odd that I always found myself thinking of Michael as quite young—about Cheryl's age—rather than almost as old as Dick Ellicott.

"Now look here, Louise Cather," he said slowly. "Do I look crazy to you?"

"Not to me, Michael," I said.

"Don't be funny. I mean seriously."

"I answered you seriously. I said you didn't look crazy. But you act it sometimes—now, for instance. Why don't you say what's on your mind?"

He leaned forward and looked silently at me for a moment. Then he said, "What shall I do, Louise?"

"The first thing I'd do is get a good lawyer."

"Archer's a good lawyer."

"You asked me, and I told you."

"You don't think he is?"

"I'd get a good lawyer who's not connected with all this."

He looked at me silently again.

"What else?" he said.

"Well, I'd quit sticking in my room brooding about something you don't know whether you did do or didn't do.

112

That's second. Third, I'd go to Lieutenant Kelly and I'd tell him everything I knew from the beginning. That's if you didn't do it. If you did do it, you'd better keep away from him. Fourth . . . well, fourth, Michael, I think something's got you down. I don't know what it is, but you don't seem to have any fight in you. You know?"

He pushed his hair back slowly and rubbed the back of his head. He looked, I imagine, as the Puritan fathers did when they were sore beset and sore perplexed.

"Look here," he said abruptly. "I'm going to tell you something, and you can tell me what to do."

"Shoot," I said, and instantly wished I hadn't. He looked a little hurt. "Sorry, Michael," I said. "Go ahead."

"Sunday night, after I sent that wire, I went to my hotel and went to bed," he said, as abruptly as before. "And *I* . . ."

He hesitated, and then went on doggedly.

"I came to, running down the hall like a fool. Nobody was around, and I got back to my room all right. It's the first time that's happened to me for eleven years. Do you see now why I'm not *sure?*"

He stopped and looked at me uncertainly; and there was fear in his deep-set eyes.

"Why did you come here, Michael?" I said quietly.

"Because I was a fool," he groaned. He got up and began to pace back and forth.

"Sit down," I said. "You make me dizzy."

He sat down again, ran his fingers through his hair and pressed the back of his neck as if there was some deep-seated pain there.

"I came because I got a letter from Agnes Hutton," he said at last very slowly.

"Oh," I said. I hadn't intended prying into his private affairs.

"I used to be engaged to Agnes. I don't know how it happened. I was going to France—I guess that was it. Well, I got back. I'd forgot all about it, and then when I was cracked up and got back here, well, it just died out. After my father's death I went out West. I heard from Agnes once in a while. She managed to keep track of me, and one day she showed up in Arizona."

"She told me that," I said. "Lieutenant Kelly knew it too."

He looked surprised.

"Well, she told me a lot of stuff about what was going on here. Trent was playing fast and loose with my share of the business. I got pretty sore. Then she left and I got to thinking it over. I decided to let it go. I didn't want to come back, and I'd done well enough out there. So I didn't do anything about it."

He started to get up, and sat down again.

"Well, when I got to New York I wrote her I was going abroad, and I was signing over my interest in Trent and Spur to Cheryl. You see . . . well, I'm not in love with Cheryl, but she's sort of a link between me and my father, and all that. I wanted her to have anything they'd left me. Well, I got a letter back saying that was fine—Cheryl was marrying Dick Ellicott in June, I owned all of Trent and Spur and it wasn't worth a damn and Cheryl could probably use the stock to paper the summer house with. That made me sore."

"I thought you didn't care?"

"Well, I don't care. But the idea of little Cheryl grown up enough to marry anybody sort of got me. It's crazy, I suppose, but once I . . . nearly hurt her, pretty badly. She didn't cry, and wasn't afraid, and I never forgot it. Sometimes out in the desert in the deep blue nights I could close my eyes and remember the flannel of her pajama sleeve around my neck, and her cold little fingers on my cheek. I'd kept on thinking of her as a six-year-old still. I guess it was the idea of her being grown up made me want to come back."

"Then you didn't want money from Mr. Trent?"

He flushed.

"Where'd you hear that?"

"Lieutenant Kelly."

"That's it, is it?" he said angrily. This time he did pace the floor. He stopped abruptly and stared down into my face.

"Does Kelly think I murdered Trent in cold blood—and does he think I did that to Agnes Hutton?" he demanded.

"I think the first is a definite possibility," I said. "And I've even heard the second mentioned."

He sat down quietly in the chair by the fireplace.

I proceeded to tell him several things. That practically everyone in the house subscribed to one or the other of the theories about Mr. Trent's murder—either he had done it walking in his libido, as Mrs. Trent put it, or he'd done it in cold blood, deliberately. Cheryl was the only person who was absolutely convinced he was innocent.

"Is that straight, Louise?" he demanded eagerly.

"So help me," I said. "In fact that's what she went into

114

your room to tell you, the other day, and you practically threw her out."

"How could I stand there and look at her, knowing I'd killed her father—don't you see?"

"Yes, I see," I said. "But I don't think she did. Why don't you come along with me, and let's talk to her about it."

He jumped up and went down to her room. She was lying on the sofa with a handkerchief folded over her eyes. She sat up and smiled a questioning, apprehensive little smile. I thought at first she'd been crying, but there was no trace of tears.

"Sit down," she said.

I told her why we'd come, and that Michael denied having anything to do with either Mr. Trent's death or Agnes's, and that I thought the two of them ought to talk it over, and then we'd see what we could do.

But she seemed to have changed since I'd seen her last. She straightened quickly, and looked at me and Michael as if she'd met us somewhere, but couldn't quite remember either where or why.

"I think Mr. Doyle and Lieutenant Kelly can manage very well," she said coolly. "It's very sweet of you both to come, but I don't think there's anything to be gained by . . . by our talking about it."

I stared at her, absolutely dumfounded. What had happened to the child? Then I looked at Michael. A dull flush had mounted his face. He got up and bowed with a sort of awkward dignity.

"I'm sorry, Cheryl," he said. "I misunderstood something Louise said."

Cheryl sat still and erect and white, staring at the door he closed quietly behind him. I stared at her.

Suddenly her eyes widened.

"Oh, Michael!" she cried, with a heartbreaking sob. She dashed across the room and threw open the door. I heard her feet pounding lightly in the deep carpet.

"Michael!" she called. "Michael!"

After a few moments she came back, broken and dejected, and fell on the floor at my feet, and buried her yellow head in my lap, sobs racking her slim body.

"Oh, Louise! What have I done, what have I done?"

"Something pretty bad, Cheryl," I said.

SEVENTEEN

I left Cheryl and went out to find Lieutenant Kelly. I met Dick Ellicott in the hall. He asked where Cheryl was and I said out in the stables, that being the farthest away of any place I could think of offhand. Fortunately when I got downstairs I found Perry Bassett standing in the hall, turning his brown hat round and round in his rough hands, apparently wondering about something. I imagined something in his seed catalogue. I told him to go up and see what he could do with Cheryl. He nodded just as if he understood the whole situation and really had been waiting there until he could help out.

Lieutenant Kelly had his horn-rimmed spectacles on and was sitting at the library table doing what he called "paper work." It consisted mostly of chewing the already much mangled end of his "*see*-gar" and spitting the proceeds over his right shoulder. He was alone, and he seemed rather glad to see me, and listened with a growing scowl that got deeper and deeper when I got to the part about Cheryl running down the hall, crying "Michael! Michael!"

"What I want you to do," I said, "is not to let Michael leave here until they come to some kind of an understanding."

"I think that's very interesting, now," he said sardonically. The cigar was virtually bitten in two at this point, so I felt justified in holding out an enormous pewter ashtray. He put the whole thing in it without thinking; thought too late, blinked at me and grinned sheepishly.

"Don't like my cigars, do you?"

"You need a good rope to chew on," I said. I took a handful of Mr. Trent's cigars out of the carved box on the table and gave them to him. He grinned again and stuck them in his vest pocket. They were still there when I saw

116

the last of him some days later. I don't know where he kept his own.

"All right, now, lady," he said seriously. "You and me can just have our talk now. Shut the door, will you, and sit down."

I closed the door and came back, and told him everything Agnes Hutton had told me, and what I'd done subsequently about getting the papers she'd left in her drawer for me to take to New York.

He fairly glowed with self-approbation during my story. I didn't understand it at first, and then it dawned on me that of course he'd expected something of the sort.

He saw what I was thinking and nodded very smugly.

"I kinda figured somebody'd try to get you to do that, if they knew you was leaving," he said. "I was going to search your bags half a mile up the road."

"I thought that was all off when you found the revolver," I said.

"It ain't the revolver *I'm* looking for, lady," he said coolly. "Now let's have a look at your papers."

We went upstairs and I showed him where I'd put them. He fished them out, and looked both disappointed and puzzled.

"That all?" he demanded.

I nodded.

He threw them down on Queen Elizabeth's bed with a grunt, and picked them up again. There was quite a packet of stenographer's notebooks—ten altogether—and several large manilla envelopes, sealed and marked "Personal and Private—Agnes R. Hutton."

"Sure that's all, lady?"

"All except the book," I replied. "I didn't have a chance to get it. It's still on her table."

"We'll just have a look," he said, and got a key out of his pocket.

When he had unlocked Agnes Hutton's door he said, "Be careful, this place ain't been done yet." I gathered he meant that the photographers and so on hadn't been there. I nodded and said, "It's on the table there."

We went over to the table. There was a row of books supported by book-ends in the person of Shakespeare at one end and Dante at the other. There were about twenty books —*Ann Vickers*, *The Cautious Amorist*, a couple of dictionaries, two thin volumes in pale old parchment, whose authorship I could guess, the *Rubaiyat*, and Rupert Brooke. But the

117

Droll Tales, bound in middle nineteenth century calf, was gone.

"It was right there last night," I said. "She must have forgot to leave it."

Lieutenant Kelly made a very rude noise. He bent over the end of the row and looked carefully at it, his hands thrust deep in his trousers pockets.

"Mind you don't touch it, and take a look right there," he said, pointing. "That thing's been moved in. See? You can see where it ain't been dusted today."

I looked, and saw what he meant. There was a faint line that showed where the book-end ordinarily rested. It had been pushed in about the width of the *Droll Tales*.

Lieutenant Kelly cocked a pale cold eye at me.

"Now that's right funny," he said.

I suppose I expected him to pull some sort of a rabbit out of his pocket in the way of immediately lining everybody up and getting the book without any more pother. But he didn't seem in a hurry.

"The boys'll be here directly, and we'll see," he said. "The family's leaving at two-thirty. That'll leave the coast clear. It's better to do these things without upsetting folks more'n you have to."

"But suppose whoever it is who has whatever you want takes it out with him today."

"I already figured that out, lady."

And then a great light dawned on me. It was just one of those rare things you don't take any credit for. "Just a gift," as the son of our butcher used to say when he carved the customers' heads in big chunks of raw leaf lard.

"Lieutenant," I said, "are you by any chance hunting for the parcel that Cheryl Trent brought down from Baltimore the day I came? She said it was her father's."

He looked at me impassively.

"Lady!" he said slowly; "why in *hell* ain't you told me this before? Where is it?"

I had to admit I hadn't the faintest idea, but I described it for him.

"Miss Trent say what was in it?"

"No."

"You see it again?"

I tried to remember. I had a faint recollection of seeing it on the library table when I was talking to Mr. Trent, but I hadn't really noticed it then. It was just one of the things I'd

118

recalled in trying to reconstruct the last few days. I certainly hadn't attached any importance to it.

Lieutenant Kelly still wouldn't tell me what was in it.

"It ain't safe for you to know," he said very seriously. "Not after what happened down there in the woods."

I felt a sudden wave of grateful affection for this hard-bitten methodical old man.

"It's dangerous for you, then, isn't it?" I said.

He grinned like an old satyr.

"That's *my* job," he said. "It ain't yours. That's the difference. See?"

Then another idea occurred to me.

"Look," I said. "What would you do if you were me——"

And then I could have bitten my tongue off. I'd started to ask him what I ought to do about the Foster estate; and I suddenly realized how very curious it would look for Dr. Sartoris to have what was in effect a sixty thousand dollar interest (taking Mr. Doyle's figures) definitely established by Mr. Trent's death. There seemed no doubt that Mr. Archer and Major Ellicott, to say nothing of Cheryl, could easily prove that Mr. Trent had been opposed to such a gift. Which made his death extremely convenient. Not, of course, that I had the slightest interest in protecting Dr. Sartoris, or trying to conceal the fact that he . . . well, that he was nothing but a sort of super-gigolo with the pseudo-scientific patter of the modern Mumbo-Jumbo who lives in Vienna. Still, I didn't want to be instrumental in hanging him.

"Well?" he said.

"I've changed my mind," I replied.

"Most women do," he said. "Only they generally say what they've got to. say first. Well, let me know when you change it back again. Now I'm going to be busy. I ain't hunting for a book, but if that one turns up let me know. Going to the funeral?"

"I don't know yet."

I thought it over when he'd gone, and eventually went up to Perry Bassett's room. He was there.

"I've got to talk to you a minute," I said. He stood aside a little reluctantly for me to come in. His room was as astonishing, in its way, as anything in the house. Like Mrs. Trent's, you could have told in a second whose room it was. So many things were scattered about that there was hardly room for the army cot in the corner. Bulbs and golf sticks, fishing tackle, catalogues, tobacco humidors, a stuffed white owl labeled "Jerry, 1910-1922," cabinets with shells and pressed flowers under glass. There was a covered bird cage hanging in the window, with a bird chirping and hopping about.

"You'd better sit down," he said, and looked around helplessly. There was obviously no place to sit. He pushed a lot of miscellaneous trowels and pruning shears off one end of the army cot, and said, "There."

I sat down and told him I was rather worried about what I should do, and thought he could advise me.

He looked genuinely alarmed, and very comical.

"Oh, dear!" he murmured. He seemed to be looking around for some place to escape to. I went on hurriedly to tell him about his sister's wanting me to arrange with the auctioneer to hold her bid above any offered for the Foster property the next day. He looked very puzzled.

"What does she want with that?" he asked.

"A sanatorium," I said.

"We don't *need* a sanatorium."

"Dr. Sartoris seems to."

"Oh, dear!" he said fretfully. "I thought Duncan put an end to that. He said the day before all this happened, that Dr. Sartoris was not to have a penny of his money."

"But it's Mrs. Trent's money, now."

"All the better reason for being careful with it."

"Quite," I said. "What do you think I should do?"

"I'm sure I don't know," he answered wearily. "You'll just have to think of something yourself. It's her money, and when she gets a thing into her head it's difficult to get it out. It's such a silly way of doing things."

"That's true," I said. "And if I tell the auctioneer what she told me, there's no reasonable limit to the amount they'll stick her for it. Unless the auctioneer happens to be a plaster saint who doesn't want to make money."

"You're wrong there—he really does want to make money. And the Fosters are his cousins too."

"Then it's absurd."

"I'll tell you," he said suddenly. "Just don't you do anything at all about it. Say you forgot it. That's what I do. I always forget things that are inconvenient to remember."

"All right," I said. "I'll do something like that."

I left him putting his tools back on the foot of the bed, looking rather more worried and more rabbit-like than ever.

"You might go talk to my niece," he called after me. "She knows what to do."

120

It was unfortunate, or fortunate, whichever way you look at these things, that I met Dr. Sartoris just then. He was crossing the hall towards Mrs. Trent's sitting room, and when he saw me he came on.

"I want to talk to you, Miss Cather," he said, and I was pleased to find that I didn't have any more of that business of my stomach, or whatever the seat of the emotions is, turning over with a sickening or thrilling plop. I met his gray calculating eyes quite calmly, in fact, and said "Yes?"

But he shook his head, and something of the old amused intriguing smile came back into his eyes.

"No," he said. "I thought I could count on you—but I can't, can I?"

I felt very like a beast, all of a sudden. But I said, "You certainly can, Dr. Sartoris. In fact, I'm going out pretty soon to buy you a sanatorium."

If I'd expected him to go into heroics of any sort, or even to act like Michael Spur, I was wrong. The smile at the corner of his mouth deepened, but it turned down, not up, and gave him an expression of amused helplessness. "But I don't want a sanatorium, Miss Cather."

"You're going to have one anyway," I said. "I'm fully commissioned to pay whatever's necessary to get it for you. When fully fixed up, according to Mr. Doyle, it ought to be worth sixty thousand dollars."

The smile left his face instantly. He was not looking either amused or helpless now. The thought occurred to me for the second time that he wouldn't be a very good person to have seriously annoyed at you.

"What do you mean, exactly?" he said.

I told him what Mrs. Trent had told me, that I was to arrange with the auctioneer to get the place at any cost.

"Miss Cather!" he said very seriously. "Mrs. Trent doesn't realize what she's doing. I couldn't think of having anything to do with such an idea. Is it too much for me to ask you not to do this thing—for her sake . . . and mine?"

Suddenly, before I knew exactly what I was doing, I said, "Dr. Sartoris, will you tell me why you came here last Monday?"

He looked a little puzzled, and then amused, and I was furious at myself for having let him get his old hold over me again, by the simple trick of appealing to me as if I were important to him. Now he was confident again, and rather making fun of me for capitulating so abjectly.

"Let me see," he drawled, a twinkle in his fine eyes "I think somebody *asked* me to come. Why?"

Having got that far I decided not to go back. I said: "I know. But *who* asked you? That's what I want to know."

He smiled again, with a fine mock seriousness that was pretty hard to overlook. Especially when I was really trying to help him out of what looked like a very nasty hole.

"It was Mrs. Trent, Miss Cather. Does that answer you, or would you like to see the invitation?"

His tone was that one uses toward an impertinent but fairly attractive child.

"I've seen the invitation, thanks," I said coldly.

He looked a little startled.

"And furthermore," I went on, "it wasn't Mrs. Trent who sent it. Does that interest you? It was Agnes Hutton. Lieutenant Kelly traced the telegram and found that out."

I was trying to be cold and matter-of-fact, but I was actually very excited and breathless. So much so that for a moment I hardly noticed the sudden contracting of his eyes. When I did I saw that he'd become instantly alert, and was thinking hard, though there wasn't much evidence of it when he smiled and said: "That's very interesting, isn't it? Perhaps I'd better be a bit more careful about getting my invitations confirmed hereafter. But I do thank you very much, Miss Cather."

He looked at me with a faint half-smile and held out his hand, and I, like a perfect fool, put mine in it and said, very heartily, "Oh, you're *quite* welcome!"

He laughed a little, and then, just as I was getting furiously angry, he became serious again.

"I really take this as a genuinely friendly act, Miss Cather," he said very gravely.

I was painfully conscious that I always managed to act like a convent-bred seventeen-year-old every time he spoke to me. I almost decided to go back to my room and practice writing, say, about a hundred times, Mr. McCrae's favorite admonition every time I started on a new assignment: "Now for God's sake use your head, Louise—that's what it's for."

EIGHTEEN

Instead I wandered downstairs, by the family wing staircase, and stopped to look at the suit of armor on the landing. It was rather like the one of the youthful Henry VIII in the White Tower, except that it had a spear in its mailed fist and was on foot. Must have cost a lot, I thought. I went on down, wondering what was going to happen to Mrs. Trent if she kept on throwing her money around on one thing and another now that Mr. Trent was gone and wouldn't be making any more. After all, there wasn't much difference between her purchases and her brother Perry's, except that you could always burn the pretty printed paper and the little slips he got in Wall Street and her stuff was practically impossible to get rid of. Anyway, I wasn't buying the Foster place; that was settled, and it was a load off my mind.

I was in the downstairs hall, where I'd only been that night I lost my head and fled from Perry Bassett when he turned out the light behind me, and left me to go backwards into the unknown or forwards past Mr. Trent's dead body. It was very dark then. It was brilliantly lighted now, with the end doors both open and the sunlight streaming in. I looked in the door at my left and saw a billiard room, with the walls all covered with heads of various dead animals, and a fine arrangement of scabbards without any swords in them over the enormous stone fireplace that had "Trent 1698" wreathed on it in cut stone.

I was standing looking at it when I noticed that someone was in the room and my eyes met Major Ellicott's across the top of the Baltimore *Sun*. He was watching me, and when I saw him he rose with a smile.

"Looks strange, doesn't it?"

"Yes."

I followed his eyes to the empty scabbards.

"I had them taken out the day we got Michael's telegram,"

he explained. "I thought there was no use taking a chance, with Emily's fancy doctor making such dire predictions."

He frowned a little. I got the impression that he wasn't really as offhand about it as he was trying to appear.

"Sit down, won't you," he went on. "I don't ever seem to get a chance to talk to you. Cheryl tells me you've been awfully decent to her. I'm very grateful to you. She's had a bad time of it and she needs somebody around."

I immediately began to revise my opinion of Major Elli-cott. He was *terribly* nice.

"Also, Perry's just told me about Mrs. Trent's latest crazy notion."

He shook his head.

"I've told both her and Sartoris that this is a rotten place for a sanatorium. At least, the kind I imagine he'd run. Not that I have anything against him—I haven't at all. But if Emily's a sample of the kind of patients he'd have, it ought to be where it's a little more exciting."

"It seems like a rather expensive venture," I said.

"Well, Emily's used to her own way. I suppose we could always add the property to Ivy Hill. There's only a couple of small farms between us, and they could be bought in."

"What would you do with that much land?"

He shrugged his broad shoulders and smiled.

"Cheryl and I could farm in earnest. Raise tobacco and stock. She's keen on horses and so am I. I'll admit it would be a sizable job."

"Mr. Archer told Mrs. Trent she really couldn't afford the place—that the estate had shrunk the way everything has," I said. "But she seems absolutely determined."

He laughed.

"Don't take old Archer too seriously. As long as I can remember he's always raised hell every time Emily's wanted to buy anything. If you listen to him we're headed for the poorhouse. There's no doubt he's perfectly sincere about it, though. He's the best friend this family's ever had, and he's honest as the day is long."

Which I thought was very odd, remembering that he was Michael's guardian with Mr. Trent, and that Michael's fortune was apparently exactly nil at the moment.

"How much is the Foster place worth?" I asked.

"You could get it for ten thousand, easily."

"Oh, really?" I said. "I'd thought of it as much more than that, and Mrs. Trent does too, I'm sure. She mentioned thirty thousand, and then said to go as high as necessary."

"She did?" he said. "She . . ."

Then he stopped and laughed again.

"Oh, well," he went on, "don't worry, they'll fight it out. I'd try to talk to Emily, but it wouldn't do any good. She buys land the way Perry buys stocks. I run about ten tobacco farms in southern Maryland and Virginia that she bought because she liked a chair they had on the porch or the calf nipping buttercups by a brook. She's a great old girl, really."

I don't know how long this would have kept up if Magothy hadn't appeared and said Mr. Archer wanted to talk to Major Ellicott in the library.

It was after lunch that I told Mrs. Trent flatly that she'd have to get somebody else to manage the Foster business for her. She said that was all right, she'd go to the sale the next day herself. I didn't see any of them again until they drove off, in two cars driven by uniformed chauffeurs. About three minutes after they'd gone another car appeared with five men in it. One of them nodded to Lieutenant Kelly, and they set out after the others. I gathered that the family were not to get far out of sight.

The cars had barely disappeared past the lake when four other men upstairs started what was the most minute police search I'd ever seen. All the places I'd picked out at one time or another as the ones where *I'd* hide a diamond necklace if I'd happened to steal one were the first places they looked in. Under the center table; in shoe bags, in the toes of slippers, in the center of the hearth broom. They looked everywhere. They practically turned inside out the rooms of Mrs. Trent, Dr. Sartoris, Perry Bassett, Cheryl and Dick Ellicott, and I'd defy anyone to have guessed they'd even been inside the doors when they were through. My room was done too —as Lieutenant Kelly politely explained, it would have been easy for somebody to get in and hide something there.

And nothing turned up. I gathered that from the heavy scowl on Lieutenant Kelly's face as he stood in the middle of the hall scratching the back of his head. He gave me an abstracted fey look out of the corner of his left eye as I passed him, but he didn't speak to me.

I strolled about for a while, looking in odd rooms downstairs and having a very nice time with the house all to myself. I could almost feel the house itself relax, now that all its tense strained occupants were gone. I knew it wouldn't be for very long, and I was quite pleased when I ran into a closet that had tennis rackets and a couple of mashie niblicks, a croquet set and a shelf of modern novels in it. I looked the books over and got one of them, and wandered outside to a grove of white and purple lilacs in full gorgeous bloom, about two hundred yards from the house. It was in the opposite direction from where Lieutenant Kelly's men were crawling about under hedges and around bushes, following the path Agnes Hutton had taken for her last ghastly journey. I found a little pool beyond the lilac grove, and a summer house where the sun sifted through long clusters of purple wisteria. There were comfortable wicker chairs there, with high backs like spread peacocks' tails, and I pulled up a foot rest, settled myself in one of them, drew a long satisfied breath and closed my eyes.

I suppose I went to sleep. When I opened my eyes the light through the curtain of wisteria was a deeper blue, and I thought at first that I must have dreamed of hearing Major Ellicott speaking somewhere not far from me. But the dream went on.

"I have a right to call you my little wife, because you're going to be, and I love you."

"I know, Dick. But it's . . . oh, I don't know. But please don't. And don't touch me, please."

"Listen, Cherry. Are you *sure* you want to marry me?"

"Oh, yes, Dick. Of course I do."

Her voice was a strange nervous contrast to the tenderness of his.

"And there's no one else, Cherry?"

"Oh, no!" she cried quickly.

"Then look," he said. "I want you to marry me now—tomorrow, dear. So I can take you away from here, and from all this horror, Cheryl."

"In June, Dick. We can't do it before."

"It's May now, June's only a month away. We couldn't have a big wedding anyway, Cherry—and I want you."

His voice sank to a whisper. After a moment he said, "There's no reason for waiting. Is there?"

She didn't speak.

"Then we'll go away tomorrow—just you and me, Cherry."

"They won't let us!" she cried.

I should have thought any man could have heard the wounded agony in that girl's voice. But poor Dick Ellicott—I suppose he was so much in love with her that he couldn't hear it; or if he did, like a man, he'd quite selfishly put it down to something very different.

126

"Oh, yes," he said. "Don't you worry about that. Doyle's coming out later and I'll tell him. He'll be tickled to death to help us."

"I suppose he will," Cheryl replied in a dead little voice.

"Of course he will. Let's sit down a while, and I'll tell you all the things I've been thinking about you for days and days."

"No, Dick," she said quickly. "I've got to go back. Really I do."

"You're always running off, aren't you? Can't you stay with me just an hour—or half an hour?"

"No, Dick—please. I can't really. I must get back. Don't touch me, please."

"All right, Cherry. Kiss me once, and you can go."

Just what an eavesdropper can do under such circumstances is a difficult question. I suppose I did what most eavesdroppers do—I sat tight and hoped to heaven they'd go before they found out I was in the chair with the high fan-shaped back. I hardly dared to breathe. After a while I saw Major Ellicott on the far side of the lake. He was sitting there smoking a pipe, one arm thrown affectionately around a shepherd dog who usually followed at his heels all over the estate. I slipped quietly out of the summer house, through the lilacs and back to the house, feeling rather sorry for Dick Ellicott, major or no major.

NINETEEN

When I came downstairs that night, half an hour before dinner, Mr. Archer, Major Ellicott, and the State's Attorney Mr. Doyle were standing together out on the terrace, talking. Perry Bassett, a little grayer, I thought, and even more than before like a frightened rabbit, was sitting close to the open window, pretending to be doing nothing and listening as hard as he could. He looked up when I came and put his finger to his lips. The three men on the terrace must have heard me, because they moved away out of sight. Perry Bassett motioned me to a chair beside him.

"They found the rest of the rope," he said in a semi-whisper. "It was cut off a coil of mine. I could have told them that. I knew it when I saw it, first thing. It was in the shed where I keep my things."

"Where's Michael now?" I asked, without any connection except a vague shapeless fear in my own mind that the three men outside constituted a definite danger to him.

"He's in his room. That man told Emily's doctor that he could go talk to him. Emily's doctor had an idea. I don't know what it was. They won't tell me. I think they ought to—it was my rope."

Perry Bassett knew one other thing too. They had found five cigarette butts tossed into the bushes near Agnes's body. They were an ordinary brand, but Michael happened to be the only person around who smoked it. The interesting thing, however, was that two of the butts had lipstick on them. Lieutenant Kelly had decided that whoever had hanged Agnes Hutton had talked things over with her first.

Perry Bassett lit a cigarette nervously.

"I don't like any of this," he said. "I wish they'd do something. You know——"

But he didn't get any farther. We heard a gay fat flutter of laughter, and saw Mrs. Trent, her left hand tucked coyly in

Dr. Sartoris's crooked arm, her large black lace hulk listing heavily to port, coming along the terrace toward the table where Magothy stood with a tray of tall frosted mint juleps. Mr. Doyle was at her other side. Cheryl brought up the rear with Major Ellicott and Mr. Archer. Her face was as waxen as the dogwood petals, and the crimson slash of her mouth reminded me suddenly of the Judas Tree.

She seemed to me to be carrying on automatically, her mind very far away somewhere, imprisoned behind a wall of ice. I noticed that Perry Bassett started when he saw her, and she came over to him at once when he and I went out on the terrace. It was the strangest cocktail hour I've ever been through. As a wake it wasn't enough, and as an event in a house whose master has been buried not five hours before, it was altogether too much. If it hadn't been for Cheryl's frozen blue wide eyes and the black crêpe heart on Magothy's sleeve, I should have thought we were celebrating Mr. Trent's departure for the Fourth of July week-end in Paris. Mrs. Trent was in fine spirits. She laughed and tapped her doctor coyly on the ear with her platinum lorgnette when he said he hoped he could get away in the morning.

"No, Victor—we're *never* going to let you go," she cooed.

Major Ellicott winked at me.

"Why not buy in the Foster place, Emily," he said, "and turn it over to Sartoris for a hospital?"

Mrs. Trent's foolish smile faded and disappeared. Her face ran through the whole gamut of emotions—or all that she was capable of: surprise, annoyance, anger and what not; and ended on a high blank note, as if she hadn't the slightest notion what he was talking about, and no interest in finding out. And she refused to be drawn. Fortunately Magothy helped her out by announcing dinner.

I don't know whether it was the mint juleps or the fact that Michael was upstairs that made Mr. Doyle quite willing to discuss what Mrs. Trent had suddenly started referring to as our cause célèbre. He told us about the cigarette butts.

"We think they didn't go down there together, because we found several places where his footsteps on the clay path were on top of hers, when there was plenty of room for them to walk side by side."

I glanced at Cheryl. Her cocktail fork had stopped halfway to her mouth; she was staring at Mr. Doyle like a snared canary at the family cat.

"Then you know?" she asked quietly, lowering her fork and controlling her voice with a great effort.

Mr. Doyle laughed.

"I wouldn't say we *know*," he said. "I really don't come in this yet. Technically speaking, Lieutenant Kelly, as a kind of special agent here, gets the evidence, and puts it in front of me. I interpret it, and I prosecute."

He leaned back in his chair, much pleased, but in a very decent way, at being here in pretty much the position of a valued friend of the family.

"Of course," he continued, "I'm pretty much interested in this case. Lieutenant Kelly's a good man, in his way, but he can't see back of things, the way the doctor here does, or if I may say so, the way I can in this particular case. I guess I've mentioned to you all about my little museum."

Cheryl looked a little frantic, and I gathered she'd heard it several times before.

Mr. Doyle turned to me.

"Now I guess that would be something to write about for your magazine, Miss Cather. I'd like you to come down and see my little collection some time. I guess that would be something new, now, wouldn't it?"

"I've been in the museum at Scotland Yard, Mr. Doyle," I said.

"Sure enough?"

I nodded.

"Well, then, you'd like my little collection. I've got the brick doorstop a young nigger boy killed his grandmother with, and I've got the piece of corset lace that tripped old Mrs. Oliver down the steps and killed her deader than Hector, when she'd put it there herself to trip her husband."

I expected momentarily to see Cheryl topple forward into the asparagus and hollandaise on her plate. Mrs. Trent seemed perfectly enchanted, and nobody else seemed to mind.

"Of course," Mr. Doyle went on, "my prize exhibit is the gun that Michael shot his father with. It was my first case as States' Attorney. I keep it and the bullet we got out of Spur's heart in a special place. I'm going to add another gun and a piece of rope to it pretty soon now."

I don't know what Cheryl thought, or even what she looked like just then. I felt a wave of nausea, and I had to look steadily down at my plate. I didn't hear what Mr. Archer said, but I did hear Mrs. Trent's reply.

"Oh, that will be all right. Victor will certify that he's quite insane."

Victor looked a little startled, I thought, but he should

have recovered instantly under the icy shower of Mr. Archer's remark that it took three doctors to certify in the state of Maryland and they had to have Maryland licenses.

Major Ellicott stepped into the breach.

"I'm sure Miss Cather would like to see your museum, Doyle," he said. "Cheryl and I might run her into town after dinner and have a look at it."

He turned to me.

"You haven't been off the place since you came, have you?"

"I think it would be a very good plan for all you young people to go to town and go to a movie," said Mrs. Trent.

There was a silence. Not even Mr. Archer seemed to think of anything to say. Then Cheryl spoke. "I'm sorry, mother," she said. "I don't feel like going to a movie tonight. I think it would be very nice for Dick to take Louise to town."

I would rather have waited to see Mr. Doyle's museum, granting I had to see it some time. But Mr. Doyle wouldn't hear of it. The idea of having his museum "written up" seemed to have got hold of him. I tried, but unsuccessfully, to explain that I had very little to do with what Mr. McCrae decided to publish.

And that explains why I was standing in the door with a black velvet jacket on, waiting for Major Ellicott to see something about his car, when Lieutenant Kelly came downstairs. He looked pretty near fagged out. I gathered that he hadn't had a particularly successful day.

Going somewhere?" he inquired, touching my jacket sleeve.

"Going to town to see Mr. Doyle's crime museum," I said. Then I added, rather annoyingly, "I'm sorry I can't wait until he's added the other gun and the piece of rope. Which I understand is to be done as soon as Michael Spur is put in a sanatorium."

"I ain't so sure that's what I'd call it," he said dryly.

I gasped at that.

"You don't mean you think Michael killed Agnes Hutton?" I demanded.

"I don't know what I mean, lady."

He ambled off just as Major Ellicott came into sight driving a Buick roadster. He got out and said, "Half a minute while I find Kelly."

"He's just gone into the library," I told him.

I had half expected Lieutenant Kelly to put a stop to our leaving. He didn't, not even when Mr. Archer decided he'd go with us. Mrs. Trent remarked, very audibly, that she hoped he'd plan to stay when he got there.

We started, Mr. Archer very red with annoyance.

"I sometimes wonder why I put up with that woman," he spluttered, mopping his pink brow. "If it weren't for Cheryl, I'd throw up the sponge, I declare I would!"

I was rather crowded over against Major Ellicott, and I caught a glimpse of his dark face in the mirror over the windshield. He had an amused smile on his face.

"I suppose you nipped the Foster business in the bud," he remarked.

Mr. Archer grunted apoplectically. "I had that out with her on the way home this afternoon," he said. "I don't want to hear it even mentioned again. But I must say," he added reluctantly, "she was more reasonable about it than I expected."

"That's because Dr. Sartoris refuses to accept it if she does buy it," I put in. I might as well have thrown a bunch of red poppies at a bull.

"What's that?" Mr. Archer demanded angrily. I told him what Dr. Sartoris had said to me. He blew his nose violently.

"So that's it," he said. "He thinks he'll get a hundred and fifty thousand out of her anyway? That's probably where——"

He stopped short, or perhaps it was Major Ellicott's sharp turn of the car that shook him into silence. He spent the rest of the trip fuming to himself. We dropped him at the post office, promised to pick him up at the home of a local bank president on our way back, and continued around Church Circle to Mr. Doyle's office at the top of Main Street.

Mr. Doyle was already there. He'd left immediately after dinner and his display was already spread out in fine style. I must say there's always something curiously unreal and sentimental to me about crime relics. The door stopper with which the sixteen-year-old colored boy had brained his grandmother (aged seventy-five) for the $2.35 she had in the old purse around her knee was nothing but a brick covered with a torn piece of old turkey carpet. It had a brown stain on one end of it, and it had sent a boy to the Cut for life. And Mr. Doyle showed me a blue steel automatic labeled "State of Maryland *vs.* Michael Spur, August 18, 1919," and a bullet in a sealed glass box labeled the same way. It was just a gun and the spent bullet was nothing but a piece of blunted lead—and yet there on Mr. Doyle's desk, with Ma-

132

jor Ellicott and Mr. Doyle and me bending over it, lay the thing that had destroyed two men, a father and a son.

The State's Attorney had that curious mania for publicity and being "written up" that you find among so many otherwise sensible people. He gave me a lot of pictures of himself at various peaks of his career, and somewhere I still have a list of his vital statistics. I was rather glad when Dick Ellicott took me by the arm and said, "Look here, Louise, you're not going to keep me here all night."

We got out, and I'm ashamed to say we went to a movie across from the State House and had a very pleasant evening. I forgot all about Dr. Sartoris—and from a number of little things that happened I rather think Dick Ellicott forgot all about Cheryl. At least when we called for Mr. Archer somewhere, and were told he'd decided to spend the night in town, Dick Ellicott grinned at me and said, "I'm glad—I like to talk to you," and I don't quite remember whether it was my knee or my wrist he squeezed by way of punctuation. Anyway, we got on very well, until he said, "You know, Cheryl and I are going to be married shortly."

I said, "Yes, I know."

"Well, do you know that for the last week I haven't been very sure that it was the wisest thing to do?"

"For you or Cheryl?"

"Both," he said. "There's seventeen years' difference in age, for one thing."

"Have you just discovered that?"

"I've just been thinking about it. And . . . well, honestly, she seems different the last week or so, somehow. I don't know whether it's all this awful business that's changed her, or what. She's just not the same."

"That's natural enough," I said.

"I guess so. Do you think she's crazy about this fellow Sartoris—the way Emily is, and the way Agnes Hutton was?"

"That's a quaint idea," I said. "I shouldn't have thought of it."

"Maybe you wouldn't," he said, giving me a queer look. "But maybe you haven't any idea of the number of times I've run across them in the summer house behind the lilac grove. In fact, that's where they were the night Duncan was murdered."

"How do you know?" I said quickly, still not quite clear in my mind as to what he meant.

"I saw them there at half-past one. He was standing up

talking and she was sitting with her feet up on the chair with her arms around her knees listening to him."

"On *Monday* night—the night Mr. Trent was shot?"

"That's right."

"What were they talking about?"

"I didn't hear."

"Jealous?"

"Maybe."

"I suppose that explains why neither of them heard the shot."

"Probably."

"But it doesn't explain," I continued, "why you and Perry and Agnes didn't, does it?"

"Or Emily, or Michael Spur, or Archer."

"Mr. Archer's a little deaf, isn't he?"

"That's right," Major Ellicott admitted. "He's the only one that's got a decent excuse."

"Mrs. Trent too," I said. "She had a mud pack on her face."

And then suddenly the car sputtered, faltered, and came to a dead stop. I looked at Major Ellicott. He was swearing softly but with considerable feeling.

"Ignition?" I asked. "Battery? Carburetor?"

"Empty gas tank," he said curtly. "I told that damn nigger to fill her up this morning. We've got a thousand gallon tank on the place and this has happened twice to me this year."

There's something perfectly futile about an automobile with no gas in it. We sat there a moment.

"How far is it?" I asked.

"About two miles. And it looks like rain. Mind?"

"No," I said. But I really did a lot. Two miles in the rain in high-heeled slippers, with a blistered heel from two miles in riding boots, is a long way, especially on country roads.

We started, but we didn't get far. A car came up behind us and stopped by the side of the road. I laughed heartily. The men in it were Lieutenant Kelly's. I understood why he'd been so willing for us to go to town, and I wondered if they knew we'd left Mr. Archer behind.

They were rather apologetic about getting caught, as it were, and explained that they'd have been closer to us but they stayed to see the end of the comedy and we left in the middle. However, they gave us a lift to the house.

As we were going in Lieutenant Kelly and Dr. Sartoris came out of the library. Lieutenant Kelly looked at his watch and strode out into the drive just as his men were parking the car. "Run me into town," he said, and I heard them rattling off in the police car.

Dr. Sartoris looked at me and smiled faintly.

"Did you have a nice time looking at Mr. Doyle's relics?" he asked.

"Very," I said.

Mrs. Trent pounced out from the living room.

"Oh, Victor, is that you! My *dear*, I thought that dreadful man was going to keep you all night. You were in there almost two hours talking to him—and poor little me all alone with Perry and Cheryl."

"You should have gone with us, Cheryl," Major Ellicott said, sauntering into the living room as I went in.

"Oh, hullo, Michael. How's the boy?"

"I'm all right, thanks. Has Kelly gone? I want to see him."

"He's just gone."

"Oh, damn him," said Michael bitterly. "I told him I was waiting for him."

His hands moved nervously through his hair, and I looked at him almost in alarm. He seemed terribly on edge.

Just then Dr. Sartoris came in from the hall with Mrs. Trent clinging to his arm, and Michael glared at them.

"For God's sake, Aunt Emily, can't you quit hanging onto that fellow—at least till your husband gets cold in his grave?"

There was an appalled silence—on my part at least.

Then Michael thrust back his forelock with a savage movement, and said, "Oh, I'm sorry, Aunt Emily. I don't know what I'm doing."

He cast a penitent glance at Cheryl and strode rapidly out of the room.

"Well, I declare!" Mrs. Trent gasped.

Cheryl, who was still sitting at the bridge table with Perry Bassett, twisted one corner of her red mouth in a sardonic half smile. "Buck up, mother," she said dryly, getting up. "Let's take a walk, Perry. I need a little air."

Perry Bassett disengaged his legs from the legs of the card table and his chair and said he'd like to. But Cheryl turned back from the opened window.

"I guess we can't escape that way," she said; "it's raining again."

135

The inquest on the body of Agnes Hutton was held the next morning. Dick Ellicott and I were the only people going from Ivy Hill, except Lieutenant Kelly, who had come back out some time the night before, and appeared, all barber-shaved and powdered and polished up and ready to go, before I'd begun my breakfast. He decided that because Major Ellicott's car was stuck gasless out on the road the three of us would go out in the police car and take some gas with us, and Dick Ellicott could drive us into town. There was some rumor that Mrs. Trent had ordered her car brought around at eleven o'clock, and he didn't want the police car to be away—apparently just in case.

I hadn't seen Cheryl to talk to, although I knew she and Perry and Michael had gone out before breakfast and hadn't returned by the time we started. I wondered if she was still planning to marry Dick Ellicott that day. I figured, however, that she couldn't marry him as long as he was with Lieutenant Kelly and me, and something might come up to give her back her courage. Dr. Sartoris, who was making short work of a large fluffy pile of flannel cakes and honey at the other end of the table, said he was happy to say Michael was better this morning. Not as overwrought as he had been last night. Lieutenant Kelly, who ate with us when Mrs. Trent wasn't down, said "Yeh?"—and that finished that.

When we left Dr. Sartoris was standing in the drive. It may have been my imagination entirely that gave him the air of a man speeding an inopportune parting guest before he went back to his own affairs. Anyway, we drove off, and found Major Dick's car. Lieutenant Kelly unscrewed the cap of the gas tank and Dick Ellicott emptied a gallon tin into it.

"That'll take us fourteen miles," he remarked, and put the tin back in the police car.

It was rather a tight squeeze. Lieutenant Kelly said he thought I ought to reduce, and laughed heartily. Major Ellicott entered into the spirit of the thing and computed our combined weight at five hundred and thirty-five pounds. My hundred and thirty was rather overpowered in the middle, and I got awfully mixed up with the gears and brakes and things when Dick Ellicott started the motor, turned off the windshield wiper, shifted in my opinion a lot oftener than was necessary, and drove us into town. We stopped at a service station at the end of the bridge, and while the man was filling the tank Lieutenant Kelly went in the shop to telephone. He brought me out a package of gum.

The inquest was brief and most perfunctory. The sheriff was present, and explained that Lieutenant J. J. Kelly of the Baltimore Bureau of Detectives was Special Investigator in charge, and then retired to a side table, where he struggled audibly with what I should imagine was a hollow tooth. Dick and I were the only witnesses immediately connected with the Ivy Hill family. We told about finding the bodies, and the jury immediately returned a verdict of murder by persons unknown, and were dismissed by Dr. O'Brien. Lieutenant Kelly later told me that he'd pulled a fast one to keep them from hanging the whole works on Michael Spur from the drop of the flag. He didn't say what the fast one was.

After that there was a sudden relaxing in the room. Lieutenant Kelly and the other out-of-town people present—they included a dozen or so reporters from Baltimore and Washington—gathered around the sheriff, and there was a lot of heavy humor indulged in. I didn't know what the joke was, but it was obviously on the sheriff; and then we were told by a young chap standing by us that Mr. Doyle's office had been burgled the night before and four half-gallon jars of ten-year-old evidence, and some other truck, carted off. As it was one of the few burglaries the town had ever had for years, it was funny in itself, but I gathered that to have the police burgled was of course immensely more so.

As we were going out I was surprised to see Mr. Archer. I hadn't noticed him come in. He nodded to me and drew Dick Ellicott off to one side. Lieutenant Kelly, seeing me standing there, came over and asked me if I'd like to see Mr. Doyle's museum in its present state. I said I would, very much. He ambled over leisurely and shook hands with Mr. Archer.

"I was goin' to look you up this morning," he said. "One

137

of my men traced a safe deposit box of Mr. Trent's. Under the name of Harrington."

"Yes?" said Mr. Archer curtly.

"Well, he found it. And it was empty. Nothing in it."

"Empty?" said Mr. Archer. The color faded suddenly out of his face, and left it the color of dirty putty.

"Yeh," said Lieutenant Kelly placidly. "Empty." He added as he turned away, "Thought I'd tell you. Thought you might like to run uptown this morning and have a look."

Mr. Archer's lips closed firmly. I saw that he was a man of good stuff; the color came back into his face.

"I'll go now," he said.

Lieutenant Kelly followed him a few paces, telling him whom to see in Baltimore.

Dick Ellicott said, "The old fellow seemed pretty shaken for a minute."

I nodded

"I'll bet he wishes Agnes Hutton was here."

"Why?"

"She knew more about the Trent and Spur affairs than anybody in the place. I guess they thought sometimes she knew too much."

Lieutenant Kelly came back just then and told Dick he was going down to Mr. Doyle's office for a few moments and that I was going with him.

"Then I'll come along," Dick said.

The sight of Mr. Doyle's office, still pretty much the way his visitor had left it, seemed to give Lieutenant Kelly a good deal of quiet fun. The cabinet that had held the museum was practically empty, and the large file that had held the four jars of ten-year-old evidence was entirely so. Papers were dumped about, and Mr. Doyle's secretary, whose name was Miss Lacey, was a very worried woman.

"It's the Ridge Beach papers I can't find," she said. "We've *got* to have them."

Lieutenant Kelly nodded affably, and when Miss Lacey went out of the room he winked at me.

"This'll keep the Big Shot busy for a month. Won't have so much time to pleasure himself around Ivy Hill."

He chuckled gorgeously, and I looked severely at him.

"Did you do this yourself?" I demanded in a whisper; but Miss Lacey was coming back, and Lieutenant Kelly remarked blandly, without any apparent relevance that I could see, "There's more ways of killing a horse than choking him on butter."

When we went out and got into Dick Ellicott's car he still seemed very well pleased with himself. We stopped at a drug store on the Circle, and while Dick Ellicott was inside I accused him again of resorting to very low methods to get rid of Mr. Doyle. Not that I blamed him much. Mr. Doyle was certainly on the side of what Mrs. Trent called "managing things." But Lieutenant Kelly was not to be drawn.

"Anyway," he said smoothly, "it's no lower than the way you're walking off with Miss Trent's feeancy."

I stared at him open-mouthed. "What do you mean?" I demanded hotly.

"Plain as the nose on your face," he said, "except that you ain't got much of a nose to speak of. But it's plain, anyway, that the major ain't looked at Miss Trent half a dozen times since you been around."

"You're crazy," I said.

"No, I ain't crazy. It's you're crazy not seeing he's crazy about you. What do you suppose he comes to town with you for?"

"Don't be absurd," I replied hopelessly.

"I ain't absurd," he said soberly.

When Dick came out he remarked, as blandly as you please, "We was just saying you must be buying out the store."

Dick Ellicott smiled at me.

"Dr. Sartoris asked me to get some sleeping powders for his patient," he said.

To get to Ivy Hill from town we had to cross three drawbridges—one over College Creek, one over the Severn, one over a little inlet about a mile this side of the road that ran down to the gates. For some curious reason Lieutenant Kelly suddenly began to take a great interest in their operation. He stopped the car while he got out and passed the time of day with the keepers of the first two. Dick Ellicott and I stayed in the car and talked, and I found it a little uncomfortable, at first. If Lieutenant Kelly thought I was trying to make off with poor little Cheryl's dashing major, what might the major himself think—and Cheryl too?

But we did get on very well together, and once he said, "I wish we didn't have to go back, don't you?" I said, very primly, that I thought Cheryl would miss him if we stayed away too long. Then he asked me how it had happened that I hadn't married anybody. That's always been something to explain. A lover lost in the war is a pretty good explanation, but the war was awfully long ago and I was only thirteen when it ended. So I said I didn't know. He said he thought we'd hit it off awfully well, and I was about to say something acidly about his scheduled elopement with Cheryl, when Lieutenant Kelly came back. Fortunately the little bridge over the inlet hadn't a keeper.

When we got back to Ivy Hill there was a man from Baltimore waiting. He had a brief case with him, and he and Lieutenant Kelly went into the library together. About two minutes later Lieutenant Kelly came out and asked me to get hold of Mrs. Trent and bring her to the library at once.

She was out in the lilac sheltered summer house, I eventually discovered, with Dr. Sartoris. I approached as noisily as I could, and when I got up to them she was standing looking down towards the water. Dr. Sartoris was doing what in a less poised and confident person would be called desperately pacing the floor.

"Lieutenant Kelly wants to see you right away, Mrs. Trent," I said. She turned around. She had been crying, and the mascara on her eyelashes had run so that she looked exactly as if she'd got a couple of black eyes in a tavern brawl.

"You must come with me, Victor."

"You'll manage better alone, Emily."

He spoke kindly but very firmly.

"But I'm doing it all for you!"

I don't like to say she sniffled, but that's just what she did do.

"I think you'd better take Kelly into your confidence, Emily," he replied quietly. "You have very little to gain, and you have a great deal to lose."

"But it's only you——"

I interrupted just then, quickly.

"I'll go with you, Mrs. Trent, when you see Lieutenant Kelly, if you want. But you must come along and wash your face, and see what he wants."

I took her by the arm, and by dint of talking continuously I got her to her room and got the mascara mopped up, and took her downstairs, protesting but subdued.

I must say I wasn't prepared for what we found on the library table, or the look on Lieutenant Kelly's face as he stood behind the table. One hand jingled the change in his trousers pocket, the other pointed sternly to the photographs in front of him. They were a dozen or so greatly enlarged fingerprints. They were all the same, and even an amateur could tell they were identical with the smaller set on another sheet, labeled "Mrs. Emily Bassett Trent."

She looked at them. I felt her stagger, saw her clutch at her throat and go the color of painted chalk. I steadied her with one arm round her waist, or half-way round anyway.

"What about it, now, Mrs. Trent," Lieutenant Kelly said furiously. "These are your fingerprints."

If a King Cobra could talk I imagine he'd have just that sort of flat cold deadly voice. I was genuinely frightened.

"These are your fingerprints, Mrs. Trent—and they were all over Agnes Hutton's room."

"I know it," she gasped helplessly. "I was there."

"Sit down," he said in the same tone. "What were you looking for?"

"Oh my God!" said Mrs. Trent. "Where's Mr. Doyle?"

"For God's sake!" said Lieutenant Kelly. "He ain't here—forget about him, and tell me what you were up to!"

His voice rose to a harsh shout, and I thought Mrs. Trent was going to faint.

"Mr. Doyle ain't going to get you off," he shouted; "what were you after?"

She clung to my arm and sobbed convulsively.

"Oh, God forgive me," she cried, "I was hunting letters."

Lieutenant Kelly's eyes flashed.

"What kind of letters?" he barked.

"I thought Victor—Dr. Sartoris—was writing her letters, and I wanted to find them. I hated her, and I wanted to know, to be sure. I saw him coming out of her room. Oh, I can't stand it!"

"When was that?"

"The night before—late. Oh, I was so unhappy."

She choked miserably.

"Then in the morning they told me she was dead, and I said I'd lock the room. That's when I went in."

"What'd you find?"

"Nothing. Nothing at all."

Lieutenant Kelly moved around the table with incredible speed and thrust a stubby finger accusingly in her face.

"Mrs. Trent!" he said slowly, "we know you took a book off her table. Where is it? And what else did you take?"

She gave a couple of convulsive sobs. And then a strange thing happened. Just as one can see air coming into an inflating balloon, I felt something—strength, or desperate courage, decision, perhaps just craft—coming into Mrs.

Trent. Her next sob rang very false, and when she looked up at Lieutenant Kelly her face was blank and vapid.

"I didn't take anything," she said. "I wanted to find Victor's letters because I knew she knew him. She told me about him first two years ago. I thought he was in love with her. But I was wrong. He didn't write her any letters, and he assures me he never was in love with her at all. She just pestered him the way women all do."

I understood exactly why Lieutenant Kelly was so pleased that Mr. Doyle was out of the way—he never would have allowed the ordeal that Mrs. Trent was put through during the next fifteen minutes. And Mrs. Trent was as adamant, so to speak, as an indestructible jellyfish; and when she was finally allowed to go and the door had closed behind her, the man with the funny little toupee who had brought the brief case down, and was sitting with it across his knees, expressed it very adequately, I suppose: "You didn't get to first base, did you, Joe?"

Lieutenant Kelly mopped his brow with a large purple silk handkerchief.

"Let's see what else you got," he said placidly.

I didn't know until later that Lieutenant Kelly was slowly getting the tangled skein of the Ivy Hill murders untangled and laid neatly across the back of a chair. For instance, though I might have guessed it, I didn't know that he'd sent Agnes's shorthand notebooks, that I'd stowed away under my mattress, to Baltimore to be completely transcribed. I didn't know that in four days he'd traced the lives of Michael Spur, Agnes Hutton, Victor Paul Sartoris and Louise Cather so that he knew as much about each of them as they knew themselves. And I was as much surprised as Cheryl was when she and I were sitting in my room after lunch, talking, and he stuck his head in the door.

"Lady," he said with a scowl, "what do you call that red stuff the Hutton woman had in her hand?"

For a moment I couldn't think what he meant, and then the picture of Agnes Hutton clutching the bruised magenta branch came with nauseating clearness into my mind. I said, "Some places they call it redbud. Here they call it Judas Tree."

"Yeh," he said. "Thanks."

He closed the door, and Cheryl shook her head.

"I wish they'd get somebody else down here," she said.

We'd been talking, Cheryl and I, about Major Ellicott.

"Sometimes I don't think I'm the person for him to marry,

142

Louise," she said. "He's so much cleverer than I am. I used to think, sometimes, that even Agnes was a better match for him than I was, as far as brains went, because I'm an awful dud, you know. But a person like you could do a lot for him. And he ought to live in town, not in the country like this. That's what Perry thinks too. You know, Perry's funny —the other day he said, 'Now your father's dead, you don't have to marry Ellicott.'"

"Your father wanted you to?"

"Yes. I don't know just why."

The most ridiculous thing flashed through my mind then. If Cheryl's father had insisted on her marrying Dick Ellicott, and Perry Bassett didn't want her to, perhaps Perry had killed him so she wouldn't have to. It seemed pretty far-fetched, and also, I reflected, it certainly didn't explain Agnes Hutton's death, even if she was hanged with Perry's rope. So I dismissed that idea and went on listening to Cheryl.

"Mother's never liked Dick very well," she was saying, "and I don't think she was very keen about me marrying him before Dad died. But now she's all for it. The sooner the quicker. I don't know why. I suppose she'd like one of Dad's wishes carried out."

"You know, Cheryl," I said, "I inadvertently heard your talk with Major Ellicott yesterday. I was in the summer house."

"Oh—really?"

I nodded.

"It doesn't matter. I've decided to wait."

I smiled at that.

"Maybe I'm just stubborn, but I thought I'd tell Mother about it. After all——"

She shrugged her shoulders indifferently and unhappily.

"There's no use being silly about such things. Well, she was all for it. It's the first decent word I ever heard her say to Dick. Wished him all sorts of nice things."

She laughed mirthlessly.

"I just had the feeling that she was saying the 'Here's your hat, what's your hurry' sort of thing, and I balked. I told Perry this morning. He didn't like it a bit. He's funny. You know, Louise, I think he'd do anything for me. He said he'd even go to town to live if we could have some window boxes."

"He's sweet," I said. "And speaking of sweet people, how's Michael Spur?"

143

She turned two wide serious young eyes towards me.

"Oh, Louise," she said, "I'm so afraid! Michael told me while you were in town that he knew my father and Mr. Archer had absolutely ruined him, but he didn't care, because he sort of thought of it as part payment for his killing his father. It was his father's money. And I talked to Victor then, and he said Michael couldn't really forgive them, he must have some deep resentment. He might not be conscious of it, you see, but it could come out in one of his spells and he'd kill my father."

"That's just the same old idea, Cheryl, isn't it?" I said. "And what's more, it doesn't explain Agnes Hutton."

She held out both her hands in a helpless gesture of despair.

"I know, but it might. Agnes told Michael about the money business last year, and she's known about it for years, you see, that they were . . . just selling him out. It was a sort of revenge she was getting, and it wasn't any revenge unless he knew about it. She knew so *much*, you see."

"Doesn't sound sensible to me," I said promptly.

"Oh, I hope not—I do *so* hope not. I couldn't bear it, Louise, for him to have hurt her . . . that way. It's so beastly cruel. She looked so awful. I'll never forget it."

She closed her eyes, and one large tear squeezed under her long lashes and slipped down her pale cheek.

"Michael was really awfully in love with her once," she said. "I remember every time I wanted to see her she was off with him somewhere, and he always told her all our secrets. I hated him for it. I thought they were so important—about where the cardinals' nest was and where I'd seen the first violets, and that sort of thing."

She laughed unhappily.

"It doesn't matter, though."

"I suppose not," I said very insincerely.

And actually it turned out to matter infinitely more before another day was over than it ever had when Cheryl was six and a cardinal's nest and the first violets were all that was at stake.

TWENTY-ONE

I went down to find Lieutenant Kelly and met Mrs. Trent standing in the hall. She seemed to have recovered entirely from her temporary lapse. She was looking at herself in a rather fine girondole that her independence of spirit had hung over a seventeenth century lowboy near the door. Her first remark was characteristic, I thought; she said, "Dear me, I'm a perfect sight, Miss Mather. Will you come upstairs while I write a note to Victor and take it to him for me?"

I started to suggest that she send a servant, but I thought better of it and went along with her.

We went through the downstairs hall to the other stairs leading up to the family wing. Mrs. Trent pointed to a lovely tapestry hanging over a carved chest and said, "That's a very fine Goblin, they tell me." She seemed to be speaking of the things we passed as if she were seeing with a new eye. In fact, she said, "You know, I never really felt like I owned this house until now with my husband and that Hutton woman always around."

I think I could almost have felt sorry for her—a little—if she hadn't immediately added, "Oh, I tell you, Miss Mather, my life hasn't always been a bed of roses."

Perry was just coming into the back hall as we got there. He'd been working in the garden. Mrs. Trent stopped short, hands on hips in a gesture suggesting long generations of washerwomen, and looked at him.

"Now I ask you," she said. "Doesn't he look like a sheep in wolf's clothing, all covered with dirt?"

In fact he did look decidedly sheepish, and very much ill at ease. She waived it all aside.

"Well, that's what he's like. He's aesthenic. Victor says they're all queer. You'd better change, Perry."

"Yes, Emily," he murmured, and stepped aside while she swept up the stairs with me in her trail.

At the landing she paused, and looked fixedly at the knight in armor.

"That piece," she remarked, "is worth more than the whole place put together. The plume was in the hat I wore when I met Queen Marie in New York."

Then she laughed, and I realized that it was the first time I'd heard her laugh, except when she was being arch and affected. It gave me a strange sensation up and down my spine for a second. But she wasn't paying any attention to me. She went on pointing out the other objects of interest in the household fittings, almost as if she were trying to sell me the place. I glanced furtively back at Perry Bassett. He was trying to hide behind an armoire, and I looked further down and saw Dr. Sartoris coming in, just as Emily Trent turned up the stairs from the landing. I was glad we'd missed him; I'd rather deliver a note than witness another scene between them.

I waited for Mrs. Trent to write at least six notes and tear each one up before she got one that suited her. She put it in an envelope and very carefully sealed it. Then she wrote "Kindness of Miss L. Mather" on the outside.

"Will you give him that, like a dear child?" she said, and smiled at me with eyes that were a thousand miles away.

Again I experienced that queer feeling up and down my spine.

She sat down at her dressing table and began to dab at her mouth with a lipstick. I got out as quickly as I could.

Outside the room I stood with her letter in my hand. There was absolutely no doubt in my mind that Emily Trent was entirely mad; and suddenly as I stood there, wondering what to do, my heart began to beat violently with just sheer fright. I was all at once just horribly afraid of the woman.

Could there be any possible doubt, I thought, not only that Emily Trent was insane, but that she was also a murderess? Like a flash there came into my mind her words in the summer house this very morning: "I've done it all for you"; and I remembered Dr. Sartoris's face. I thought back over the nightmare of the last four days. If any human being ever thought she had a motive for murder, Emily Trent thought so. She was afraid of both her husband and Agnes Hutton; she hated Agnes, probably her husband as well. There was no doubt also that she had some sort of mad obsession about Dr. Sartoris—call it love if you wanted to. I suppose it was that. Or passion flaming up in a thwarted and unhappy woman who was getting old. Those two people stood in her way—kept her from what I suppose she thought of as happiness.

Her mud pack the night of Duncan Trent's murder could have been a fake. The story of Michael Spur's psychosis was largely her story. She kept it alive. She could have used it as a mask for her own murderous designs. Supposing Agnes *had* got Sartoris down to Ivy Hill, and supposing Agnes *had* sent the wire for Emily Trent when they learned Michael was coming. Mrs. Trent, I knew well had her full share of a sort of low animal cunning—she could have arranged it. She could have shot Duncan Trent. She was the last person downstairs. Perhaps her brother knew it, and that was why he had hid the gun in the flower bed. If I only knew why she took the book!

Agnes's death, coming after she'd seen Dr. Sartoris coming out of Agnes's room, seemed too awfully clear. Suppose the woman had got rid of her husband, throwing the suspicion on Michael Spur, only to find that her doctor was deceiving her with her husband's secretary, whom she hated. She couldn't, I suppose, know, and I should perhaps have told her, that Dr. Sartoris had come from Michael Spur's room, and met Agnes and me at Agnes's door; that he hadn't really been in her room at all.

There was only one thing I couldn't possibly fit in. Mrs. Trent could never have walked as far as the spot in the dogwood copse where we found Agnes. She could of course have had an accomplice.

I don't know how long I might have stood there, stupidly holding the letter in my hand, weaving that dreadful network of guilt around the woman behind me—probably still making up her flabby face—if Dr. Sartoris himself hadn't appeared, suave and serious, and stopped in front of me.

"Is it as overwhelming as all that, Louise Cather?" he inquired lightly.

I looked up at him. He wasn't smiling; he was deadly cool and unsmiling.

"Yes," I said almost mechanically. "Yes, it's very overwhelming."

He calmly took the letter out of my hand and put it in his pocket.

"Thank you, Miss Cather," he said. He bowed and went back toward his room.

My first impulse was to run after him and tell him what I thought. And then I realized that I couldn't do that. I must find Lieutenant Kelly.

I turned and ran downstairs. Perry Bassett was on the landing coming up. I don't know where he'd been all the time, except that I noticed his shoes were cleaner. He looked at me with a perplexed little frown.

"Are you ill?" he asked tentatively.

"Oh, no!" I said breathlessly. "I want . . ."

Then I realized that I mustn't tell him either, and I ran on downstairs. "No, I'm not ill!" I called back up after me, and made a dash for the library door.

Lieutenant Kelly looked up and took off his horn-rimmed spectacles with ponderous deliberation.

"Calm yourself," he said.

I realized later how funny it would normally have seemed. But I couldn't be calm then. I told him what I'd discovered. He listened. When I'd finished he shook his head.

"Listen, lady," he said. "Mrs. Trent's a buzzard—she ain't an eagle. She goes around and picks up what's left behind. She ain't going out and *do* nothing."

He got up and came around to where I was standing, and put his big paw on my shoulder.

"Now listen, lady," he said, patting me with a sort of rough kindliness. "I'm right worried about you. It's that red head again. Now, you either got to stop thinkin' about this, or I'm goin' to pack you off home."

"Why?" I demanded.

"Why? Well, I'll tell you. You're going to run into something, if you don't watch out. Listen—there's somebody around here that ain't going to stop at *nothing*—you hear? Now, this job is my job, and I'd give a nickel if you'd never got your pretty red head *in* this business. Now, I gotta hunch that if you stay outa things, you're all right. Will you, now?"

"I'm not *doing* anything," I said.

"No, but you're thinking too much, and there's no telling when you might do something. You quit it. Forget about it."

I had to laugh a little at the idea of forgetting it.

"Lieutenant Kelly," I said, "will you tell me this? Do you still think Michael Spur had anything to do with it?"

He looked at me a long time, his white lashes almost concealing his shrewd old gray eyes. He went quickly and silently to the library door and threw it suddenly open. The hall was empty. He closed it carefully and came back.

148

"Listen, lady," he said quietly. "I'll make a bargain with you. I'll tell you just what I think about that young fella, if you'll keep what I tell you to yourself, and if you'll go and stay with Miss Trent and do fancy work or jigsaw puzzles or something till I get things cleared up around here. Is it a bargain?"

"Yes. It's a bargain."

"O.K. Then I'll tell you the low-down. I don't think young Spur had any more to do with it than I did. I think somebody's using this what-you-may-call-it . . ."

"Psychosis?"

"This psychosis idea to pull the wool over our eyes. They pretty near got away with it on account of Doyle being interested in psychology. If your uncle J. J. Kelly hadn't of come on the scene, well, they'd had him in a straitjacket somewhere, and they all would a been sitting pretty—except the little gal. Then Hutton gets in somebody's road. That branch of the red stuff was somebody's idea of a joke, lady. Well, I guess Judas was one of the world's best little double-crossers. And our friend Agnes wasn't a slouch at it."

I simply stared at him.

"Now you hold your horses, lady, and you'll find out soon enough. And you can take it from me that the fellow that done this is nobody's fool. And the Trent woman is. Now you run along and don't forget that bargain."

On my way upstairs to find Cheryl I realized that the sum total of all he'd told me was practically nil. Nobody but a too complete half-wit would possibly believe Michael Spur had committed those two horrible murders in an unconscious state. Nevertheless, when I got upstairs I saw there was a man sitting on a chair just outside his door. That Michael himself was in Cheryl's room, as I soon found out, and that the two of them had their heads almost touching over an elaborate jigsaw puzzle of Washington Crossing the Delaware, seemed beside the point.

Cheryl raised a flushed face and bright blue eyes.

"Come in, Louise," she said. "Michael's got all of one soldier done."

I looked down on part of a disembodied head of the father of his country, and Michael looked up with a friendly grin.

"You do his cape, Louise," Cheryl said.

"That's not a cape, that's a cloak."

"It's not either, is it, Louise?"

There was a tap at the door.

"Come in!" Cheryl called impatiently.

The door opened and Dick Ellicott looked in. "Oh, hello; busy? I thought I'd get you to play a set of tennis with me."

"Oh, I'd love to, Dick, but we're just on Washington's cloak, and I *couldn't* leave. Louise, why don't you . . ."

Major Ellicott grinned at me.

"Fine!" he said, and Michael Spur said, "That's an idea!"

"I haven't played tennis since last summer," I said when we were going downstairs.

"All right, let's not play. Let's just talk. I've been hunting all over the place for you."

Lieutenant Kelly was standing out on the terrace. He shook his head at me and grinned. Dick Ellicott and I strolled toward the lilac grove. It was a gorgeous day. Neither of us said anything until he said, "I suppose Cheryl told you she'd broken our engagement?"

"No," I said. "When?"

He took a piece of note paper from his pocket.

"I got it before lunch."

He held it out to me. I shook my head.

"I'm awfully sorry," I said.

"I'm not," he replied. "Not honestly. Cheryl's a grand girl, but I don't think it would have worked."

"You're lucky if it doesn't make any difference."

"Well, that's just the point," he said slowly. "It does make a lot of difference . . . to me, Louise."

I don't know whether I was glad or sorry when Perry Bassett appeared, looking very cheerful about something, and talked to us steadily until Dick looked at his wrist watch and said we ought to be getting back, if we wanted a cocktail before dinner.

TWENTY-TWO

A yellow cab in the drive was in the act of debouching the gray and pink rotundity of Mr. Thomas Archer when Perry and Dick and I came through the opposite door from the garden.

"Oh, dear!" said Perry Bassett. "My sister thought he had gone for good."

"I hope not," Dick remarked. "Not while he holds the family purse strings still."

Mr. Archer gave us the most perfunctory greeting. He wanted to see Lieutenant Kelly, and apparently he wanted to see him bad; and Magothy hastened to conduct him to the library with as much ceremony as if he hadn't practically lived at Ivy Hill for fifteen years.

The man in the hall in front of Michael Spur's room was gone. I decided perhaps that meant Michael was in his room, since he'd been out of it while the man was sitting there. I went into my own room and dressed, and got to thinking —forgetting, of course, part of my bargain with Lieutenant Kelly. Somehow the business of Dick Ellicott seemed to complicate matters, and I wasn't very happy about it. And the more I thought about it, the more unhappy I got; and before I'd finished dressing I'd decided clearly and firmly that there was just one thing in the world I wanted, and that was to get away from this awful place and get back home.

Something like a wave of nostalgia went through me— nostalgia, and relief at the idea that I *could* go home. I looked around. If I could get away right after dinner, I could take a night train up, and in the morning I'd wake up in the noisy peacefulness and safety of the Penn Station, and be hundreds of miles away from this nightmare of lilacs, and sunshine, and dogwood, and murder.

For the next few moments I acted more like a maniac

myself than a sane woman. I got a lot of things together and got out my bags. I didn't pack them, I hadn't time; and furthermore, I thought I ought to see Cheryl before dinner and tell her I was leaving. I rushed out of my room and down the hall to hers happier than I'd been for a week, as if I were Atlas suddenly freed from the burden of the world. I didn't bother about knocking even, but burst in. Then I stopped short. Mrs. Trent, in an incredible pink velvet peignoir, was standing over poor Cheryl, simply giving her hell! Cheryl, frightened and as white as wax, was crouched back against her dressing table. I saw Mrs. Trent's face reflected in the mirror. It was positively livid with rage. She had a piece of paper in her hand and was shaking it angrily at the girl.

"You *will* marry him! I'm not going to have you ruin my life! I've waited years for this, it's not going to be snatched from me!"

Cheryl's eyes, catching mine, suddenly changed, and her mother looked up and saw my reflection in the mirror. She turned quickly.

"*You* talk to her, Louise Mather! *You* tell her she can't do this!" she cried.

Then her wrath subsided like a pricked bubble, and she sat down, exhausted by the fury of her emotion.

"Tell her what, Mrs. Trent?"

"Tell her she's got to marry Dick. I *planned* on it. I can't leave her here alone!"

She sobbed miserably.

Relief and anxiety struggled in Cheryl's voice. "But, mother!" she said. "You're not going . . ."

"I'm not going anywhere!" said Mrs. Trent hastily. "But I want you settled. You've no right to go back on your promises. Your father's heart was set on your marrying Dick. You ought to consider *his* feelings. You tell her, Louise."

Cheryl looked at me and shook her head.

I spoke up anyway.

"Don't you think, Mrs. Trent, that this is a pretty bad time to decide anything as important as that? I'd wait a little."

"But I want her settled, so I can get away myself. You know yourself, Cheryl, I've been a virtuous *prisoner* in this house for six months. I can't leave you here alone, after everything that's happened."

"Well, mother dear," said Cheryl patiently, "if you have been a virtual prisoner here it's your own fault. You can go. I can stay here—Louise will stay with me."

I groaned inwardly.

"Well, I never," exclaimed Emily Trent brightly. "I never thought of that. So she can! Well, now? Maybe she'd like to move her room. You ask her, Cheryl. Oh, dear, I must rush and get dressed for dinner."

She sailed out of the room as if nothing had ever bothered her in all her life. Cheryl, still white and shaken, sank down in a chair and closed her eyes. Neither of us could think of a word to say—at least, I didn't dare say any of the many things I was thinking. After a few minutes Cheryl sat up and made what seemed to me a definite understatement of the case.

"Mother's rather unstable," she said simply.

I sat down and laughed until I cried.

I got control of myself after a minute, said "I shouldn't wonder—I'll see you downstairs," went back to my room and put my things away again. All I thought was that I couldn't leave the child until I saw what was really up— and incredible as it sounds, I hadn't the faintest idea of what Mrs. Trent was actually planning.

Downstairs Lieutenant Kelly seemed to be directing all sorts of operations from the library. People came and went; and across the hall, subdued but fairly coherent, the family life of cocktails, dinner and bridge went on. The only allusion to the late unpleasantnesses was made when Magothy announced that Mr. Archer was having his dinner with Michael on a tray. Mrs. Trent had apparently not heard that he was back. She surveyed the room through the lorgnette and said, "I should think he *wouldn't* eat with decent people. He's a whitened sepulchre."

Perry Bassett said, "I should think Michael would be the last person in the world he'd want to be with."

It was one of the very few public speeches I heard him make.

His sister said, "You don't know anything about it," and that ended that. I caught Dick's eye and looked the other way.

We were finishing dinner when Lieutenant Kelly appeared and stood behind my chair.

"I'm asking you folks to be careful," he said. "I'm doing the best I can to protect you. One of my men'll be on duty in the house tonight, and as long as I think it's necessary. I'm telling you all that, so you won't be scared if you run into him, and I don't want nobody to shoot him by mistake. We'll have everything cleared up pretty quick now, but I got to ask you all to be on guard."

There was a thoughtful silence after that. Not even Dr. Sartoris seemed able to think of much to say.

About nine o'clock Magothy came into the living room and told Mrs. Trent that Mr. Archer would like to see her a few minutes. "I'd like to see him too," said Mrs. Trent firmly. Cheryl, who had been playing double Canfield with Dick Ellicott, got up and went out with her. Dick came to our table and took Mrs. Trent's hand. He and Perry took the next three rubbers from Dr. Sartoris and me before Mrs. Trent came back.

"Well, that's settled," she said, and sat down again; but her mind, never entirely on her game, was even less so now, and we broke up after a few hands. In spite of Dick's masterful playing Dr. Sartoris and I were something like 98 ahead of her and Perry. Cheryl came back as I was saying good night to Mrs. Trent. She kissed her mother and Perry Bassett, and we went upstairs together.

I left her at her door.

"Michael's terribly upset about something Mr. Archer's been telling him," she said. "You *will* stay with me, won't you, if Mother should want to get away?"

"Yes, Cheryl," I said. "Good night."

I said good night too to Lieutenant Kelly's man, sitting out in the hall in front of Michael's door, and then went into my room. I locked the door and went over to look out the window. It was a lovely night; a clear warm moon made everything look just as if a hoarfrost had formed.

"She's right," I thought. "The whole place is a whited sepulchre."

But I decided not to change my room. I'd got used to Queen Elizabeth's bed at too great cost to give it up. In fact I'd got so I slept quite well.

I don't know how long I did sleep. When I woke up, sharply and fearfully, it seemed to me as if somebody had taken a knife and slashed a great gash in the very fabric of sleep, and left me instantly conscious of some awful naked reality. It was still dark. I sat up in bed, trying to think what it could have been that had come and gone again. Then there came a high piercing shriek that ended in sharp utter silence.

I was out in the hall in a split second. Ten feet from Michael's door Lieutenant Kelly's man lay in a heap on the floor. No one was near him. I rushed over and touched him —his hand was quite warm; I could hear him breathing heavily. I ran to the end of the hall. A light sprang up there, and I almost fell over Dick Ellicott. He was lifting Cheryl Trent up in his arms. His face was white.

"For God's sake, Louise, get Kelly!" he said quickly.

I looked back down the hall. Dr. Sartoris was running towards us, and Perry Bassett behind him. I started down the stairs.

"Not there!" Dick shouted.

But he was too late. I staggered back. A great wave of nausea went over me, and I clung to the banister.

Half-way down the stairs lay Emily Trent. She was dressed for the street, with hat and gloves. Her blood had already dyed her white crêpe blouse a living crimson. But it wasn't that. It was the spear, still thrust there, as a bayonet is thrust. In the corner of the landing stood the knight, his mailed hand still raised in its eternal gesture; but the hand was empty.

TWENTY-THREE

The rest of that night is a confused dreadful nightmare, in which Lieutenant Kelly's grim face, drawn and gray, appears to me now, as I remember, out of the darkness of the lower hall. He had had no sleep the night before, and had lain down for a few moments on the library sofa. I remember staggering back upstairs and seeing Perry Bassett on his knees by the man on the floor.

"He's been drinking," he said.

There was a sudden shout down below. I ran back to the top of the main stairs, and got there just in time to see Michael Spur stagger into the downstairs hall, his dressing gown torn, looking ill and dazed, and to see Lieutenant Kelly's men close in around him. I went on down. I remember telephoning to Mr. Doyle, and waiting for him and Dr. O'Brien in the foyer at the other end of the house. And I remember Dr. O'Brien coming downstairs again, looking rather white, and saying it reminded him of once when he was in Venezuela.

It was I who found the inert figure of Lieutenant Kelly's other guard huddled under a chair in the dining room, a glass and a decanter on the table in front of him. I was there when Lieutenant Kelly came in, bent over him, and got up with an oath. "Somebody get that butler," he said curtly. "Have him dose these men with black coffee strong as he can make it." And it was I who trotted off towards the kitchen.

They arrested Michael Spur. Lieutenant Kelly ordered Dr. Sartoris, Mr. Archer, Perry Bassett and Dick Ellicott to go into the library and stay there until he sent for them, and he ordered me upstairs to stay with Cheryl. Dr. O'Brien had given her an opiate. She was lying on her bed white and still. A man came in, locked the bathroom door and looked in the closets. "I'll be outside the door, miss," he said, and

156

went out. After a little he opened the door and Magothy came in with a pot of chocolate and some wafers, and set them down without a word. His face had the queer livid hue of the terrified darkey.

I drank the chocolate, and my head seemed a little steadier. I knew now that there was someone in this house who was not sane, and that it was not Emily Trent. It could only be Michael Spur. No one else, I remembered, knew that he had ever used a spear as a bayonet. Cheryl had said she'd never told anyone. I thought I must ask her when she woke up. She moaned and turned slightly away from me, as if she were dreaming what I had thought.

But where was Emily Trent going? She was dressed in a suit and hat and gloves. That question kept coming back into my mind, and I didn't dare believe the only answer that seemed logical. Had Michael found her by accident, or had he known she would be there? What had happened to the men Lieutenant Kelly had put in the house to guard us from just this thing?

I was sitting by Cheryl's bed when the first gray streaks of dawn turned pink and gold, and I got up and put back the curtains. The dozen solutions of the Ivy Hill murders that had seemed so plausible when the sky was dark seemed grotesquely fantastic now that day had come. I came back to the bed and looked down at Cheryl. Her eyes were open. For a moment I thought she was dead, they were so fixed and staring. I touched her hand, and she closed it over mine.

"I guess he did it, Louise," she whispered. "I believe it, now."

I couldn't say anything, try as I would.

"Will they hang him?" she asked in the same soft whisper.

I shook my head. They *couldn't*.

"They'll say he's insane," she went on pitifully. "But he's not, Victor will say so."

She closed her eyes. I rang for the maid. The policeman at the door put his head in.

"Have them send us something—coffee," I said. "And get Mr. Bassett."

Perry came. Cheryl rushed into his arms. When I went out he was smoothing her hair and saying, "There, there, little cherry blossom."

I got dressed and went downstairs. Dick Ellicott was down, and Dr. Sartoris, both dressed. Mr. Archer was with Mr. Doyle, they said. And we had a rapid new development. Mr. Archer was furious at the arrest of Michael Spur—they had no evidence, he said. What had stunned Michael was his jump out his window. Lieutenant Kelly's men had locked him in. When he heard the screams on the landing he had tried to get out, and when he couldn't he had jumped out the window. His dressing gown had caught on an iron awning hook, and he had fallen and been badly shaken up.

While we were standing there Lieutenant Kelly came in; he had several strands of black and white flannel in his hand.

"All right as far as it goes," he said grimly. "Looks like a straight story."

Burns, the man I'd found in a heap on the floor, had come around. His story was simple. Mrs. Trent had brought him a pink flask of what she said was pre-war stuff, and had told him to take it to help him stay awake—because she was so alarmed. He had not thought anything of it, and the sleepier he got the more he had drunk, until he felt himself slipping. He had tried to get downstairs to his mate on guard there. He had no notion of what time he had passed out.

When the other came to, we got the same story from him, except that he had been presented with a decanter by Mrs. Trent.

I was with Lieutenant Kelly when he went upstairs to Mrs. Trent's room. When he opened the door I got my first glimpse of it since her death. Three bags were packed and set out in the middle of the room; her hand bag and a light coat of summer ermine were lying across the yellow chaise longue. In her fireplace there was a little heap of charred paper, and a young man was on his knees in front of it, carefully picking out the larger flakes.

Lieutenant Kelly strode directly into Mrs. Trent's bath-room and opened the medicine cabinet. There was a pill box on a lower shelf. He read the label. It was dated the day before, and had Mrs. Trent's name as the patient and Dr. Sartoris's as the physician. I saw Lieutenant Kelly's jaw tighten as he opened the box, but it was manifestly quite full. He scowled and put it back. Then he picked up an empty bottle, also issued to Mrs. Trent, and dated three days before —the day of Mr. Trent's murder. I saw the words "Not to Be Refilled." The doctor's name on it was J. J. O'Brien. Lieutenant Kelly held the bottle carefully and removed the stopper. He smelled it, then moistened his tongue with a drop still remaining, and nodded with some satisfaction.

He started to turn away when something else caught his eye. I looked too. There were two bottles of aspirin on the shelf, one half full, the other empty. Lieutenant Kelly scratched his head and scowled again. Then he carefully put the empty bottle by the aspirin bottles, took a roll of adhesive tape off the top shelf, closed the door and plastered it shut with the tape.

"I don't want anybody in there just yet a while," he said.

When we went back into the bedroom the man at the fireplace looked up.

"Parks says they've got some stuff down there," he said. "They went through the doctor's room with a fine-tooth comb—nothing doing."

My heart sank very stupidly. I went along with Lieutenant Kelly. I felt, and I dare say I looked, as if I were tagging him around, but I wanted to ask him about Michael Spur and he didn't give me a chance. He looked too grim and formidable, and I knew he was desperately worried. I don't know where he ever got so many men all of a sudden as seemed to be around, taking pictures and doing other things in a perfectly matter-of-fact routine way.

Two men were in the hall whom I'd seen the day before. One of them had a canvas bag, and he said "Here you are, chief." They put it down on the floor and opened it. It was a rather soggy mass of papers and miscellaneous objects, and I recognized one of them at once. It was the carpet-covered brick I'd seen at Mr. Doyle's museum. There were a couple of revolvers there too, one of them of a rather unusual shape, and I thought I recognized it too. I glanced at Lieutenant Kelly.

"Where'd you find it?" he said.

"Under the bridge, the little one," said one of the men. "Guess they got away with the liquor."

"Take it away," said Lieutenant Kelly. I very brightly halted their going by saying, "But where's the other gun? Michael Spur's gun."

Lieutenant Kelly turned and glowered at me through his white stubby eyelashes. He hesitated a moment. Then he said curtly, "I got hold of that before the burglary. You boys give that stuff to Doyle. Get going."

I stepped back, feeling a little miffed. Lieutenant Kelly's manner had been rather short, and my nerves were decidedly ragged. I stepped on somebody's foot and turned quickly and said, "I'm sorry!"

I saw Perry Bassett standing there just behind me, looking very blank. He nodded absently at me and said, "Lieutenant Kelly, has anyone found my sister's will?"

159

"What's that?" Lieutenant Kelly said very quickly. "Your sister had a will?"

"Yes," said Perry timidly. "She made a will. Mr. Archer will tell you."

Lieutenant Kelly raised his head like an old fire horse at the sound of the bell.

"Mr. Archer!" he shouted, and Mr. Archer came out of the living room.

"Yes?" he said.

"What's this about that will?"

Mr. Archer nodded. "It's quite simple," he said. "I have it."

He took a folded piece of legal-looking paper out of his pocket and read it, all of us standing there open-mouthed, listening. The provisions were simple, as he had said. Emily Trent willed and bequeathed her brother Perry Bassett $10,-000 cash and a return ticket to New York. The rest of her property, real and personal, she bequeathed entirely to her lawfully wedded husband. That was all there was to it.

Mr. Archer stopped and looked at Lieutenant Kelly.

Lieutenant Kelly ran his distracted fingers through his crisp white curly hair. "Well, I'm *damned*," he said. "The woman's husband was *dead!*"

I glanced involuntarily at Dr. Sartoris, and I noticed that everyone else had done the same. He shook his head and smiled. "There's some mistake, gentlemen," he said.

If there's a destiny that shapes our ends, it was certainly getting in some first-rate licks that morning. The words had barely left Dr. Sartoris's mouth when I heard the tinkle-tinkle of a bicycle bell, and saw a messenger boy put on his brakes and hop nimbly off onto the porch. He took off his hat and pulled out an oblong yellow envelope.

"Mr. Archer, sir," he said.

We all stood silently watching Mr. Archer sign his name in the small book. The boy saluted and rode off. Mr. Archer's hands shook a little as he tore open the envelope. He read the telegram. His face suddenly went purplish-red and he gave a very violent snort indeed, and handed the telegram over to Lieutenant Kelly. I looked around his shoulder and read it. It was, on the whole, the most amazing telegram I've ever seen.

THIS IS TO TELL YOU THAT I HAVE AT LAST FOUND PERFECT HAPPINESS STOP WHEN YOU GET THIS VICTOR AND I WILL BE MAN AND WIFE STOP YOU HAVE ALWAYS HATED ME TOM BUT I FORGIVE YOU STOP TRY AND RETURN THE MONEY YOU STOLE FROM

MICHAEL SPUR STOP WE CAN NEVER BE COMPLETE TILL WE LOSE
OUR LIBIDOS IN THE ULTIMATE STOP TELL LOUISE MATHER TO STAY
WITH CHERYL STOP THE GUEST TOWELS ARE IN A HUTZLER BOX
IN THE THIRD FLOOR LINEN CLOSET STOP TELL CHERYL AND PLEASE
SEE YOURSELF THAT PERRY DONT GO OUT WITHOUT HIS HAT STOP
HE WILL GET SUN STRUCK STOP I HAVE PLENTY OF MONEY STOP

It was signed "Emily Sartoris."

The silence in the hall was so dense that it was simply
deafening. I had the most overwhelming and insane desire to
giggle. Mr. Doyle broke the silence. He said, "Sorry, Kelly,
but you'll have to arrest the doctor."

I don't know what happened after that. I was so stunned
that I went up to my room and sat down, and smoked ten
cigarettes, one after another.

I sat there thinking it over, and realizing that I should have
known it from the beginning. A man who had been chief of
police in Washington once told me that ninety-five per cent
of all crimes are very simple and easily solved. Only five per
cent are even mysteries—like the Phantom Murderer who
kept shooting people down on the streets, apparently without the slightest motive. But find your motive, he said, and
you've got the five per cent too.

Dr. Sartoris's motive was simplicity itself. Mrs. Trent was
giving him money for his hospital, and Mr. Trent had put his
foot down. How long he had worked on Mrs. Trent with
his story of Michael Spur I didn't know. Mrs. Trent had said
it was Agnes who had brought them together. It was simple
to kill Duncan Trent, possibly with Agnes's help, and then
put Michael Spur, for doing it, in the hospital that Duncan
Trent's money would then build. Then Agnes—by the evidence of her own lips, from her own statement to me—
welshed; and Lieutenant Kelly had seen the significance of
the branch of Judas Tree in her dead clenched hand.

From that point on too, it was all clear. Mrs. Trent had
made her will leaving the property to him, and he had
finished his game with a master stroke. Only, he had not
given Mrs. Trent credit for being as crafty—or as stupid—as
she was. She had so arranged it that as long as he wasn't her
husband, he didn't get her money. He probably had no way
of knowing that; he had probably thought that the papers
he'd burned in her fireplace were all that remained to incrim-
inate him. He could never have thought of her final dramatic touch of the telegram to Mr. Archer.

I supposed they couldn't make men as marvelous-looking as Dr. Sartoris without there being some flaw in the golden bowl. Then I stopped short: golden bowl seemed to bring something to me. Dr. Sartoris had not got the money by her will—but I wondered . . .? I sat there thinking until my cigarette burned close to my fingers and brought me sharply to my senses.

Mrs. Trent was murdered not far from the landing of the stairway leading to the family wing.

With the suddenness of a miraculous vision I recalled her standing there, talking to me, and her strange laugh when she'd said that the suit of armor on the landing was worth more than anything in the house. I remembered her wire and its last sentence: "I have plenty of money."

It all came to me in a flash, and without thinking in the least of Lieutenant Kelly's warning, I slipped out into the hall. No one was in sight. I didn't know where they had taken Michael Spur, or even if they'd released him now that they had arrested Dr. Sartoris. I went quickly down the heavily carpeted hall to the staircase just outside Cheryl's door. The guard had gone from there too. A heavy rope had been hastily tied across the top step, to keep people from using the stairs; but the landing was empty, except for the shining figure with the gay pink plume in his helmet, and his empty fist stretched out before him. The photographers had come and gone, and with them the fingerprint men. There was a dark splotch on the lower step where Emily Trent had fallen.

I glanced over my shoulder at Dr. Sartoris's door at the end of the vertical hallway, and slipped under the rope and down the stairs, avoiding the dark splotch on the carpet.

The landing was about ten feet wide and twenty long. The knight in armor stood on his low mahogany pedestal off the rug in the corner across from me. I looked down the lower staircase. The doors were open, but no one was in sight and there was no sound.

I touched the armor gingerly. I hadn't the faintest notion how one got inside the thing. Finally I discovered a lace, and my fingers trembled nervously while I untied it and moved the breastplate enough to put my hand inside. That didn't help much—there was a shirt of chain mail under it. "Pierce both plate and mail" kept running through my head, and half my mind was trying to remember where I'd read that, and the other half trying to pull the thing aside. Then I felt something lodged tightly in between the back plate and the breastplate, and as I moved the breastplate with my arm I felt it give a little. It seemed to be a box.

My heart was beating like a trip hammer; and just then I heard a sound. I looked frantically up and down the stairs, but no one was in sight.

I had hold of the box by now; and simply *making* myself work slowly and carefully instead of just yanking desperately at the thing, I got it down, and finally, by pushing up the mail shirt, I pulled the box out into the space between the steel plates. Then I saw what I had, and my heart suddenly gave a sickening plop. It wasn't a box full of Mrs. Trent's money. It was Agnes Hutton's large calf-bound copy of the *Droll Tales* of Balzac in French.

I was just holding it in my hand and looking stupidly at it, as one does something one's been handed and doesn't know just what to do with. And then I opened it, quite unconsciously, as I would any book—and stood perfectly aghast. It wasn't a book at all, or rather it wasn't a book any longer. Its leaves had been glued together and hollowed to make a cigarette box out of it. There was the fly-leaf, the title-page and half a dozen pages of the text, and then a white sheet of paper that had been pressed tightly down to keep something underneath tightly in place. It was a letter, not folded but pressed in full length, and at the head I saw the name of a well-known Baltimore bank. It was addressed to Mr. Trent, and dated the Saturday before his death. My eyes swept quickly down the typed sheet.

"This is to inform you," it said, "that your name has been forwarded to the United States Treasury in compliance with the orders of the Treasurer of the United States, as one of our clients who has received gold and gold certificates within the last two years. We have informed the Treasury that you have received $200,000 in gold certificates. We wish you to understand that we are acting in accordance with orders received from the United States Treasury Department, and that we have no choice in the matter."

Fascinated, I lifted the edge of the letter, and saw beneath it a tightly compressed pile of yellow bills. I saw the "1000" on the top one. And then I heard a sound, this time unmistakable, and looked up. It was Perry Bassett. He was coming out of Cheryl's room, and I started to say, "Look, Perry, what I've found!" when something in the way he was moving stopped the words on my lips, and the wild insane glitter in his gentle brown rabbit's eyes literally froze me in my tracks.

"Drop that book, Louise Cather," he whispered intently. "Drop it! Drop it this minute!"

They say a drowning man lives over a complete finite stretch of his life as he sinks into infinity. In the moment that I stood there, powerless to move, with Perry Bassett creeping towards me with a living devil in his eyes, one gnarled hand pointing down at me, the whole mystery of Ivy Hill dropped into place at last, like the last miraculous piece of some jigsaw puzzle.

Mild little Perry Bassett, with his two passions: his niece and his gambling. Both taken away from him; his niece forced to marry Dick Ellicott, himself forced to potter about with plants and flowers when he knew he could make a fortune in Wall Street if they'd only let him. In my hands, between the calf-covered boards of an old book, lay everything he dreamed of or could hope for. Both he and Mrs. Trent had known the book was not a book at all, but a box to hold something that Agnes Hutton had not let out of her hands. Perry had seen her with it and had followed her that morning, not knowing she had left it behind. It was his rope that had hanged her. Everything had pointed to him so plainly—but he was so gentle and so sweet.

He was coming towards me now . . . to get the book that his sister had recognized on Agnes Hutton's table. The whole thing flashed clearly into my mind, in perfect form and harmony. It was after that that she had made her plans to buy the Foster place and to buy Dr. Sartoris. Perry had guessed it; he knew her. No wonder he was kneeling by the prostrate guard in front of Michael's door saying "He's been drinking"—when his sister was lying on the stairs dead.

Perry Bassett was half-way down the stairs, whispering something frantically. Then only the dark wet patch where Mrs. Trent's blood had soaked into the carpet, and the twenty feet of the landing, separated us; and I clutched the book tightly and tore myself away, and ran for my life down the stairs. He was running after me. I got over the rope at the foot of the stairs. I must get to Lieutenant Kelly, I thought desperately. The house was wide open, no one was in sight. I dashed through the door into the drive, and stopped for one frantic moment, not knowing which way to go. Then as I looked wildly about I saw a broad back going down the walk toward the garages, and my heart leaped, and I tried to call out for help. It was Dick Ellicott. He didn't hear me, and I started to run towards him.

I heard Perry Bassett behind me then. "Drop it!" he was

crying, "drop it, Louise Cather!" And I ran on. "Dick!" I called. "Oh, Dick!" But he hurried on, and I realized that my voice was not making any sound but a choking gasp. I ran faster. I could hear Perry's feet pounding on the drive behind me—and then Dick Ellicott turned suddenly around, and I heard Perry stop. I turned quickly. He was running back into the house. I ran on.

Dick Ellicott was standing just outside the garage door.

"For God's sake, what is it, Louise?" he said.

"Oh, take it!" I said, and I thrust the book at him.

He took it without a word, and looked stupidly at it for a second, and I looked at him. His face was very white, and there was a light in his eyes that I've never seen in anyone's before or since.

Then he laughed suddenly.

"Thanks, Louise!" he said. *"I've killed three people to get this."*

He slipped the book suddenly under his left arm, his hand went into his pocket and out, and I saw the blue-black revolver in it.

"I like you," he said. "I don't want to kill you too. Will you stay there for five minutes? Promise?"

I nodded dumbly, petrified with terror.

He gave me a quick smile and dashed into the garage. I heard the starter whir and stop, whir again, whir and stop, and I heard the pounding of heavy feet behind me and turned to see Lieutenant Kelly running desperately up the drive, with other men behind him. And then I heard the starter whir and stop and Dick Ellicott curse; and then he came out of the garage door and stopped, looking at Lieutenant Kelly. The blue-black revolver was still in his hand.

Lieutenant Kelly walked slowly towards him.

"Give up, Ellicott," he said quietly. "Put that gun down. You can't get away."

Dick Ellicott looked at him silently.

Then he said, "I imagine you're right."

He looked at me with the same quick smile, stood there white-faced and erect for an instant, and raised the revolver to his head.

I closed my eyes, but I heard the shot, and I heard Dick Ellicott fall.

Someone touched my arm, and Perry Bassett's voice, plaintive and very worried, said, "I don't think you ought to stay out here any longer, Louise."

"Take her in the house," Lieutenant Kelly said gruffly.

TWENTY-FOUR

I took the news to Cheryl. She was sitting in front of a card table, automatically putting pieces of colored wood together to finish the picture of Washington Crossing the Delaware. I think she was still too stunned to know just what she was doing. Her eyes were wide and serious, and I noticed that her fingers trembled as she picked up the pieces of her puzzle and tried to put them in places they couldn't possibly go in.

"It's all over, Cheryl," I said in as matter-of-fact a voice as I could manage.

"Over?"

"Yes. It was Major Ellicott, Cheryl. And he's shot himself."

She looked at me as if she hadn't really heard me. And then she nodded.

"That's what Perry thought," she said. "He told me so this morning."

"Perry?"

"Yes. He said it had to be Mother or Mr. Archer or himself or Dick. It had to be somebody that knew all about the other time, when Michael killed his father. I guess we both thought it was Mother and Dr. Sartoris, until last night. I know I did. Where is Dick?"

"He shot himself," I repeated.

"I'm glad," she said. She went on dully picking up pieces of her puzzle.

"I've got to do something, Louise, or I'll go crazy," she whispered pitifully.

I drew up another chair and we sat there in silence, fitting together the prow of a wave-tossed boat. I had the curious feeling that Cheryl and I were doing in odd-shaped pieces of painted wood what Lieutenant Kelly had been doing downstairs in the purple pieces of the life-stuff of the people of Ivy Hill.

When Cheryl spoke it was about her mother.

"Poor dear," she said. "She didn't understand. I talked to Victor about it, the night Dad . . . died. He was worried, because somebody had wired him to come, and Mother denied she'd done it. He was afraid she was losing her mind. I guess he thought she'd shot my father. That's why he wanted to get away. I tried to talk to Mother, and so did Perry, and she was all right until Agnes died. Then there was no holding her."

I told her about the money then. I'd forgotten it before. The other thing seemed so much more important.

She nodded.

"Perry thought something like that explained why Agnes sneaked away, and why Mother was so sure of herself all of a sudden—and why Lieutenant Kelly was here, too."

All that became clearer late that same afternoon. Perry persuaded Cheryl to take her puzzle downstairs. Dr. Sartoris seemed to feel that it had a definite therapeutic value. He said they used them in children's hospitals in psychotherapy. Michael was in the living room when she came in, perfectly poised and as white as the dogwood petals that Magothy had put in a deep jade bowl on the center table. A little smile moved in the blue depths of her eyes. I went outside.

Dr. Sartoris was lounging in a wicker chair on the terrace, gazing down the long garden towards the bay, where a white-sailed catboat moved lazily across the horizon. He looked up and smiled. I sat down wearily. Neither of us said anything.

After a little Mr. Archer came out.

"Lieutenant Kelly has something to say to you people," he said, and we got up and went inside.

Michael was sitting across the card table from Cheryl. They seemed to have got as far as the bandaged head of one of the rowers. When Lieutenant Kelly came in, looking very serious and badly in need of sleep and a shave, Cheryl looked up listlessly and rested her hands on the middle of the puzzle. Perry Bassett moved his chair closer to hers. She gave him a fleeting grateful smile.

"I ain't going to say very much," Lieutenant Kelly said. "I just want to clear up a few things. The only people that know the real truth about all this are dead. But Major Ellicott killed Mr. Trent because Mr. Trent knew something about him and was going to tell it. I'll get to that later on. And he killed Agnes Hutton because she knew he'd killed Trent, and she was going to squeal. He didn't know she had the money when he did it, is my guess. The only person he killed on account of that $200,000 was Mrs. Trent. He guessed about the money when he heard the safe deposit box was empty, and he knew it when Mrs. Trent was so cock-sure about herself. And when Mrs. Trent pulled a fast one and doped my men, with a bottle of whiskey that she'd put sleeping stuff plus aspirin in, and made first-class knockout drops of, then she gave him his chance.

"She was planning to elope that night, and Ellicott got her when she was making a getaway, expecting to meet the doctor here in the garage. Well, I was watching Ellicott. I had one first-rate piece of evidence against him, but I didn't have what you could call a motive as strong's I had against half a dozen other people."

He glanced around, and I noticed that Mr. Archer had slipped quietly out of the room.

"For instance," he went on, "I guess there ain't no use trying to pretend that Mr. Archer wasn't mixed up in some pretty shady business about Michael Spur's money. But that ain't my business. That's up to Mr. Spur and Mr. Doyle."

Michael Spur spoke up quietly.

"Mr. Archer and I have decided to fix up the business again, lieutenant. So I guess that's all right."

Lieutenant Kelly nodded.

"O.K. with me," he said. "And I guess Mr. Doyle won't be hurt. Well, now. Mr. Archer had plenty of reason for getting rid of Mr. Trent. Trent had all the money. Archer knew all about the business of Michael Spur twelve years ago. Agnes Hutton knew all about that, and all about the business juggling—and I figured, when she took the rap, that Archer might have just stopped her because she knew too much.

"Well, if anybody'd told me the whole truth, I might have got onto it sooner. For instance, if Miss Cather heard that shot, there wasn't no living reason why everybody else shouldn't have heard it—except Michael Spur. He'd had a drink or two, and if the whiskey in this house ain't a night-cap it ain't *nothing*. I guess Ellicott fixed it up for him—because he had to be kept quiet. That was just sense.

"So, what's the answer? The answer is, everybody else did hear it—and they thought they'd just better keep their mouths shut. Then, Miss Trent and Dr. Sartoris were out in the garden. The gardener said he cleaned up there around seven, and the two of 'em were in sight until twelve—and there were a dozen cigarette butts out there. The doc finally

told me about it. Then, somebody was in the library between the time Miss Cather ran through it, when Mr. Bassett turned off the light, and the time Bassett and Ellicott
came down. It's my guess that was Hutton. I know she
came down afterwards, got the keys out of the drawer
where Archer'd put 'em, thinking it was Spur had done it as
a gift from God for him, and got everything she wanted,
including that little package of two hundred thousand in
gold certificates. So then, she saw a way she could slip outa
the whole business. She was too thick with Ellicott; maybe
she planned to double-cross him from the beginning.

"She knew about it, all the time—she'd got Spur to come
here, and she lined up the doctor on the job with his psychology. She hadn't counted on Miss Cather showing up and
always getting in the way. She and Ellicott were playing
for big stakes—but the stakes didn't happen to be the same.
She was after the money. He was saving his own neck and
she knew it. And that's why Duncan Trent was killed and
why Agnes Hutton was killed, and Mrs. Trent was killed
just because she happened to get hold of the money."

He looked around. I'd heard a car drive up, and Magothy
was waiting in the door with a package. Lieutenant Kelly
nodded to him. He brought it over and put it on the table,
and then retired to a point behind the curtains where he
wouldn't miss anything.

Lieutenant Kelly turned to me.

"That night—Monday—when you happened to come
downstairs, you said you heard voices in the library. I
thought at first maybe it was the radio, but I guess it was
Trent telling Archer and Ellicott they could go to blazes.
You see, he'd made a queer decision—he'd decided to come
through clean, more or less. He and Archer were in one
thing together, but in another he had the goods on Ellicott.
Well, they heard somebody come down, and Ellicott slipped
out and stood with his back to the window, pushing his hair
back the way Spur does. They're about the same size, and
you didn't know either of 'em well enough to tell the
difference. But you sure had me going, trying to fit that in
with the rest of it. Of course, that was Ellicott's game—he
had to pin it on Spur, and that gave him a swell chance.

"Well, the break came when Doyle's museum was robbed.
I knew that was going to happen—or I guess I'd better just
say I guessed it would. I was hot-footing it in town after
Archer. Miss Cather and Ellicott and me went out to where
his car had got stuck—and the minute we started up I knew

Ellicott was the guy I was after. I guess you noticed that, lady?"

I looked perfectly blank, and shook my head.

"Well, now. When he started the car, his windshield wiper started going back and forth fifteen to the dozen. Well, I had a guard at the gate to keep cars from going out. And it hadn't been raining when you came in from the movie, had it?"

"No," I said. "It didn't start for quite a while."

"That's right. Well, somebody had been somewhere in that car when there wasn't supposed to be any gas in it, while it was raining, and came back and got out in such a hurry he didn't notice he hadn't switched off the wiper. And when we were starting off, Ellicott just reached up and turned it off, quick like. He'd have said something about it if somebody else had had the car out, and I was scared to death you'd notice it and say something about it. So I got out at the service station and phoned back to the house for 'em to get busy. They found somebody had thrown a gas can over in the bushes and somebody'd emptied a lot of gas on the road the night before. Well, I figured either he'd got away with what I was hunting for, or something else. When the old lady started bleating about paying fifty thousand dollars for a fifteen thousand place, I figured it was something else.

"What was it? Well, Major Ellicott had slipped in town and had a shot at Mr. Doyle's museum."

He was being maddeningly deliberate about it, but he had a rather strange air of plugging away doggedly at some point or other, and I waited for him as patiently as I could.

"And I'm going to tell you all something. You can make fun of psychology if you want to, but I'm handing it to the Doc here. He knew Spur didn't do these things. He told me. When Miss Cather and Ellicott were in town that night he said to come in the library and talk to him. Well, I was pretty suspicious about the story he'd fixed up about Spur, and the fact that he'd known Hutton, and then it was her that had introduced him to Mrs. Trent and so on, and that made me figure maybe the hundred fifty thousand dollar hospital they talked about was going to be his cut."

I glanced over at Dr. Sartoris, and saw that he was smiling with genuine appreciation. Mincing matters was certainly not one of Lieutenant Kelly's many excellent qualities.

"Well, now. That night he said to me, 'Lootenant, that young fella never committed murder. I been probing his libido, and murder ain't there, and that's straight.'"

I'm very much afraid I laughed. Dr. Sartoris's words sounded even worse in Lieutenant Kelly's mouth than they had sounded in that of his late disciple Mrs. Trent.

"Well, I got to thinking about that, and I said, 'Thanks, Doc,' and he said 'That's all right, it's an interesting case.' I guess that's what he thought about it. I thought it was plain hell. So I went to town, and I came back. The next morning I went to town, and that's when Ellicott's windshield wiper started wiping like it was mad."

He stopped suddenly and untied the parcel in front of him. We all leaned forward. Even Cheryl moved her head and opened her eyes, blue and wide.

"Well, now," Lieutenant Kelly said. "What was that all about?"

He hesitated, as if he were not quite sure of what was the best way to go about something; and it seemed to me suddenly as if there was something very dramatic and touching in the air.

"Why did Major Ellicott pretend his car out there was crippled, and then sneak out and burgle Mr. Doyle's museum?—I'll just show you, because it's rather interesting."

He began to take things out of the parcel that Magothy had brought in.

"Now this here's the gun that Michael Spur used that night fourteen years ago," he said, holding it up. "It's this gun that branded him, in the eyes of the world. I'm just going to call this gun Exhibit A."

He put it to one side on the table.

"And this here, this is the bullet they took out of Stephen Spur's body. We'll just call this Exhibit B."

He put the little lead pellet by the revolver on the table.

"And this here's the bullet that killed Duncan Trent; and this is Major Ellicott's service revolver—and we're going to call them Exhibit C and Exhibit D."

He placed a second little lead pellet and a second revolver on the table by the others. We watched him silently. I didn't dare to look at poor Michael Spur; and you could have heard a dogwood petal fall, it was so silent in that room.

"Well," Lieutenant Kelly said deliberately, "Dr. Sartoris was right when he said there wasn't any murder in Michael Spur. In nineteen-nineteen they hadn't found out how to fingerprint bullets. They couldn't tell what bullet came from what gun. But we can do it now; and I just thought it might be a pretty good idea to have it done here. *And I'm telling you the bullet that killed Michael Spur's father never came from Michael Spur's revolver.* Exhibit B and Exhibit C—the bullets that killed Stephen Spur and Duncan Trent—were fired from Major Ellicott's revolver, Exhibit D. One of 'em was fired fourteen years ago, and one of 'em was fired four days ago—but they was both fired from the same gun."

We sat there speechless, staring at the whitehaired old man, standing there unshaved and weary, clothed with the simple dignity of Justice.

And then he came round the table and put his hand on Michael Spur's shoulder.

"Son," he said gently, "you never killed your father."

There was an instant's breathless silence. Then Michael gave a great sob, and his hands groped blindly across the scattered pieces of the jigsaw puzzle for Cheryl's, and he dropped his head in her cool cupped hands. She bent forward gently, her face radiant, her eyes as clear as blue heaven, and kissed the top of his bent head.

"Michael dear!" she murmured, and he held her hands very tight.

Lieutenant Kelly blew his nose violently with his large purple silk handkerchief.

"Well," he said gruffly, "I guess there ain't much more. Ellicott told Miss Cather he'd killed three people. He could of said four. I had them test the bullet we took from his own body—it checks with Exhibit B and Exhibit C. And that's why Dick Ellicott had to get into town that night and get the gun and the bullet out of Doyle's museum. That was evidence aginst him that they'd been holding there for fourteen years. Doyle didn't know it—hadn't any way of knowing it at the time, and he just hadn't thought of it since.

"Well, this Ellicott had got in a bad way, and when Miss Trent wouldn't marry him he was just about desperate."

I thought with almost a blush at this point that I'd rather misunderstood Major Ellicott when he said Cheryl's breaking her engagement meant a lot to him. It just goes to show how conceited women are—I'd thought he meant something else, not that he had to get money by hook or crook or take a chance on starving as well as hanging.

"He didn't have any money, and he had a lot of expensive habits. Then, when Mrs. Trent got married, he'd be outa luck all round. Well, I emptied all the gas tanks in all the cars, just in case. And when I said I had the gun from Doyle's office he knew the jig was up. He'd thrown all the stuff from the bridge down here. Thought he might of thrown it from one of the big ones, but there was keepers there. That

172

was just a chance, now, but he had to do something with it. He was getting ready to make away with the money, if he could find it, and without it if he had to. And then Miss Cather just up and took it to him. I was watching him, so I didn't have no time to watch her too; and he'd gone into his room and out the window, the same as Mr. Spur did last night.

"Well, I guess there ain't anything else."

And Magothy appeared with a tray of tinkling frosted juleps with sprigs of mint sticking gaily out of them. He offered the first one to Lieutenant Kelly. It was as high a tribute as the old darkey could manage, being, as Mrs. Trent had once remarked, very particular about the amenities.

"If you don't mind, I'd rather have a glass of nice cold beer," said Lieutenant Kelly.

"Yes, *suh*," said Magothy.

That night I was sitting out on the terrace looking at the mantle of the stars hanging low over the shimmering bay, and watching the lights of the Virginia boats, somewhere out there between heaven and sea. Cheryl and Michael were finishing the head of the soldier in the very stern of the boat. Perry and Mr. Archer were in the library figuring how much a week in New York would cost before the market sky-rocketed, as Perry thought it would any moment now if he didn't get his $10,000 invested.

"My sister left me the ticket back home, you know," he said at dinner. It seemed to me the one last gracious thing Emily Trent had done.

I heard someone coming out on the terrace behind me. A tall shadow rested over me a moment, and Dr. Sartoris drew up a chair and sat down. He didn't say anything. The tiny gleam of his cigar lighted his face now and then. After a long time I felt him looking at me.

"Do you still think I'm a dirty dog, Louise Cather?" he asked quietly.

I didn't answer.

"I stayed on here tonight because I wanted to explain a few things to you," he went on. "In the first place, I didn't believe Mrs. Trent when she said she hadn't sent that wire asking me to come down. I thought she was just being coy and elusive. I *was* interested in Michael—and I still hold to my theory about shell shock, although I'd never have mentioned it if I'd known he was coming back. It was purely . . . shall I say, academic. After all, one had to have something to talk to Mrs. Trent about.

173

"I came down here first to see Perry Bassett, at Mrs. Trent's request. I'd met Agnes in Bermuda a year or so before. I got Perry grounded in his garden. He'll come back to it after he's had a week or so in New York. Well, I recognized in Mrs. Trent the usual symptoms of a middle-aged woman with nothing to do and a great deal of money to do it with. The sanatorium was her idea from the beginning. Now I'm afraid I wasn't above taking the hundred fifty thousand dollars and making her a patroness of the hospital—but it couldn't be down here. And as soon as Mr. Trent was killed I realized it was time for me to clear out.

"That letter you gave me, or that I took away from you, was in the nature of an ultimatum—elope and get the Foster place, or nothing. The letter Lieutenant Kelly found in Ellicott's pocket was my reply to Mrs. Trent. Ellicott had got hold of it, in some way, and she never got it. That explains why she went on with her plans, and why I was not a party to them. I want you to understand that."

"Why did you stay? And why did you let her think you were going to marry her?" I asked. Not that it made any difference to me at all, although I'm afraid my voice sounded rather as if it did.

"I had to stay, Louise. First, because after Trent's murder the police wouldn't let me go; but before that, when Trent ordered me out, the thing had already begun to look like a cooked up job on me and young Spur. After I talked to Michael the first time I began to see that the boy had never been a very acute nervous case in his life. And the more I talked to him the more I came to see that the thing that was haunting him and pulling him back to this place constantly was a deep unconscious—if you'll allow me to use the word —conviction that he *hadn't* killed his father.

"If any of you had told me the story of his stopping before he drove the spear into Cheryl, years ago, I'd have had more to go on. I suspect that somewhere in Spur's soul there's the knowledge that the shot that killed his father came in a spurt of fire from somewhere beside him. I also suspect that the information sent him by Agnes, that Cheryl was about to marry Ellicott, was what roused all those latent fears. It was that that sent him out at two o'clock in the morning to wire the Trents he was coming to Ivy Hill. Agnes Hutton tried to get him here in December and failed. He didn't care about the money. She succeeded when she guessed that Cheryl meant a lot to him. Partly because he'd nearly killed her once, I fancy."

174

"I'm surprised Lieutenant Kelly paid any attention to your theory about there not being murder anywhere in Michael's unconscious, or his libido, or whatever the two of you call it."

I glanced sideways at him. His glowing cigar showed his face in the night.

"Lieutenant Kelly's an unusually bright fellow," he said with a smile.

"Well," I said, "I suppose that clears everything up. Doesn't it?"

He tossed his cigar out into Perry's reconstructed tulip bed.

"It leaves just one thing, Louise," he said, leaning forward. "You've got to believe me when I tell you I never had the remotest intention of marrying Mrs. Trent. I'm no saint, but I'd never marry a woman for money. Marriage is something very different in my mind. I've never met but two women I wanted to marry. One of them was drowned on the *Lusitania*. The other . . . well, she literally knocked me off my feet the first time I ever met her."

I felt my heart doing one of its queer double back-flips. I suppose it must have been my libido sinking into the ultimate that Mrs. Trent talked about that told me it was me he meant . . . until he leaned forward, and I felt his hand on mine and heard him saying softly, "Louise, I love you!"

I've not been able to decide which surprised me most, his saying that, or my saying—and I can still hear my voice, quite calm and impersonal— "Let's wait, shall we, until we're back in New York. Then I'll know whether it's really you . . . or just the lilacs and the dogwood, and the stars, and . . . all that sort of thing . . . you know?"

He smiled.

"Yes, I know," he said gently. "And I'll wait, Louise . . . as long as you like."

And I did write a success story when I got home again—only it was about Lieutenant J. J. Kelly of the Baltimore Bureau of Detectives.